For Katherine and Andrew

Chapter 1

The odd thing was that when they talked about it afterwards no one could recall ever having laid eyes upon the book before that fateful morning. Where it came from was a mystery. Mum did admit, when pressed, that she just might have scooped it up accidentally with an armful of cookery books at the Christmas Jumble Sale. But she couldn't be sure. And anyway why, if that was the case, had no one noticed it during all the intervening months? It was a bulky book, bigger than all the others on the shelf and according to Katie (who was the one who found it) you couldn't miss it in the middle of the bookcase.

Anyway, the fact is that nobody did remember seeing it until after Katie had made her shocking discovery in the sitting room that Sunday morning...

A little before seven a.m. the peace and tranquillity of number 17 Mulberry Avenue had been rudely interrupted by a series of banshee-like wails coming from downstairs. Dad, whose custom it was to sleep in late on Sundays, had come to with a start, sat bolt upright in bed and, finding himself awake, chucked the duvet off in rage.

'What in the name of sanity is going on downstairs? Who's that caterwauling?'

'It's Katie.' Mum was already heading for the door, pulling on her dressing gown as she went. On the landing Josh and Andy, still half asleep, stumbled, shell-shocked, towards the stairs.

They found Katie in the sitting room, slumped in misery on the floor. Mum dropped down on her knees beside her. 'Whatever is the matter love?'

The answer was a burst of sobs.

'Tell us why you're bawling can't you,' said Andy, 'now you've woken everybody up.'

Mum pressed a wad of tissues into her daughter's hand. 'Blow your nose love.'

Katie ignored the tissues. Eyes and nose streaming, she gulped back her tears. 'He's dead!' she wailed and started to weep again.

There was a swift exchange of glances over her head. 'Who's dead?'

'Freddie! Poor, poor Freddie!'

'Oh is that all?' Josh snorted and flung himself down on the sofa.

'But he can't be,' said Andy, 'we've only had him a week.'

All eyes turned towards the big glass bowl on the sideboard. But indeed, there seemed to be no doubt about it, Freddie was floating, sideways up, on top of the water. He was definitely dead.

'There, there, love, never mind,' soothed Mum. 'We'll get you another one – maybe two – and a lovely big tank to put them in. Wouldn't that be nice?'

But Katie didn't seem to think that would be nice at all. Mum's sympathetic words were drowned by yet another wave of weeping. 'N...O...O...O! Don't want another one! Want Freddie!'

'Well, you can't have him,' snapped Dad. Having despaired of ever getting back to sleep Mr Ridley had come downstairs to deal with things himself. 'The fish is dead. And that is that.'

'Yeah,' smirked Josh, putting his feet up on the sofa, 'like the one you had with chips last night. Only you weren't upset about that one were you?'

There was a brief pause as Katie considered this remark. Then the dam burst.

'That was COD!' she shrieked, going dangerously red in the face and proceeding to howl at twice the previous volume.

'Josh, how could you!' scolded Mum. 'What an awful thing to say!'

'Cod. Goldfish. What's the difference?'

'Apologize to Katie. That was most unkind.'

He shrugged.

'Go on!'

Josh mumbled something inaudible at the ceiling. Then, sulkily: 'She's such a baby.'

'Yeah,' said Andy, agreeing with his brother for once, 'more like four than seven.'

'You be quiet!' said Mum. She was really angry now. 'One more word from either of you and you'll be sorry!'

She turned and glared at her husband. 'And you're as bad. No consideration at all for Katie's feelings.'

Dad looked a bit abashed. 'Well...I mean...' he faltered, 'the fish is dead. If she doesn't want another one what would you suggest we do? Have it stuffed perhaps? Or preserve it in formaldehyde? I mean... what can we do...?' His voice trailed off.

And then, quite suddenly, so did Katie's too. Like turning off a tap she just stopped crying. Her face became a mask of calm. But her eyes were wide with excitement. She looked as though she'd had an inspiration.

'You've just reminded me of something,' and she was smiling now – almost beaming – at her father, 'something we've been learning about at school. I know what we can do to help poor Freddie.'

'Well that's good news,' said Dad. 'Now maybe some of us can go and get a bit more sleep.'

'We'll give him a funeral,' she announced. 'A special funeral to send him to the afterlife.'

'That's a wonderful idea Katie,' Mum said brightly. 'The boys can dig a hole in the garden and we'll pop him in and say a little prayer. Is that the sort of thing you had in mind?'

'Not exactly,' said Katie.

***

All was quiet in the Ridley household over breakfast. But not for long. Dad, who had been prevented from having his usual kipper out of respect for the deceased, munched sulkily on his toast and marmalade. He reached across the table for his spectacles. The Sunday papers sat in an inviting pile in front of him.

Opposite sat Katie. She was making drawings on the box that Josh's new trainers had come in. It was with great difficulty that she had got it off him. It had a cool, fluorescent logo on it and he had been keeping his DVDs in it at the time.

She had stuck plain paper over the logo. Now she was busy covering the box with pictures that she was copying from an old book she had propped up in front of her. When the box was finished she would fill it up with all the things that Freddie would need in the afterlife: pebbles from his bowl; what was left of his packet of fish food; his little castle; his water plants; the jam-jar she had brought him home in. She knew that Freddie wouldn't exactly need the jam-jar, she had told Mum, but she thought it might have a certain sentimental value for him.

She had wondered whether Dad would be cross about the handkerchief. (But Mum had told her not to worry.) It had been one of his new Irish linen ones that she had cut up into strips. She hadn't felt it would be respectful to use one that he'd already blown his nose on, even if it had been washed and ironed. The bandaging had been the tricky part – fiddly and slippery – but in the end she thought that she had made quite a good job of it really.

'What in the name of...?' Dad was staring into his open spectacles case. He gingerly drew out a tattered parcel that rapidly began unravelling itself.

'What is a *dead fish* doing in my spectacles case?' He glared at Katie but she was quite unfazed.

'I'm trying it out for size,' she said. 'I thought it would make a good coffin for Freddie. But I had to make sure it'd fit him when he's all bandaged up.'

'Bandaged up?' Dad surveyed the heap of linen scraps. 'Is that one of my handkerchiefs?'

Katie ignored the question. 'He really ought to have his insides taken out and put in special jars – but Mum said she wouldn't do it and Andy promised to but now he won't and I don't want to either so it's just going to be the bandages...'

'Do you mean to say the whole family has been encouraging you in this gruesome exercise?' Dad looked appalled.

'Not me!' protested Josh. 'Mum made me give her that trainers box and now she's ruined it with her stupid little drawings!'

'They're not stupid!' said Katie hotly. 'And it's not a trainers box. It's a sarcophagus.'

***

No one much liked the idea of having a mummy in the garden shed but in the end there was nowhere else to put him. Katie insisted that Freddie was not to be buried in a hole in the ground and Mum drew the line at having him back in the house.

'He'll start to stink in a few days,' said Dad, 'and then we'll have every cat in the neighbourhood round here.'

'Oh, she'll lose interest in him before that, you'll see,' said Mum. 'Then we'll pop everything in the bin and she'll be none the wiser.'

But Katie didn't lose interest. On the contrary, every day after school she went to visit Freddie and had a little chat. Five days went by and next-door's cat took to sunning itself on the shed roof.

On Friday Katie had a swimming lesson. She had been trying to get her backstroke right for weeks and, as she explained afterwards, she thought it might be a good idea to talk to an expert on the subject.

'That girl's beginning to worry me,' said Mum, as she watched Katie disappearing down the garden. 'In that shed for ages every day. It isn't healthy. What does she do in there?'

'She sits and talks to herself…oops sorry…talks to the fish,' said Josh.

'She's all right Mum,' said Andy, 'she's still a bit sad that's all.'

'Sad's the word,' said Josh.

'It's only because we haven't got a proper pet,' said Andy. 'If we had a dog and it died you wouldn't be surprised if she went and visited its grave would you? Like when you go and take flowers to grandpa at the cemetery.'

'Don't start that again!' Mum flung the potatoes into the sink and began peeling furiously. 'With three kids and a job I've got no time to take a dog for walks!'

'We'd do it!'

'*Oh* yes,' Mum's voice had that familiar sarcastic ring. 'You didn't even remember to feed the flipping fish.'

'That was only one day and it was Josh's turn,' said Andy. 'How was I to know that he'd forget?'

Josh frowned, opening his mouth to protest – a full-scale row was in the offing – when suddenly all three were transfixed. From the bottom of the garden, shattering the peace of a perfect summer's evening, there came a scream fit to freeze the blood. A moment later, and for the second time in a week, the Ridley family went hurtling to the rescue.

Chapter 2

Katie had sensed that there was something wrong even before she got there. The door was wide open and the cat had gone. And then there was the smell…

Hesitantly she stepped inside and immediately capped her hand over her nose. There was the stink of something rotten in the air. She waited until her eyes adjusted to the gloom. Everything was as it should be. The flowerpots and seed trays were stacked neatly on the shelves on the far wall. The hose hung on its hook. The forks and spades stood in the corner. All seemed to be in order. And yet she felt uneasy. The three-legged stool was not where she had left it yesterday. It lay on its side against the wall as if it had been thrown there. Beside it the mower had freshly cut grass still clinging to its blades. Gav, who sometimes came and did the garden on Friday mornings, must have come and mowed the lawn. Was it him who'd gone and chucked it there?

A sudden breeze freshened the stale air, rippling the cobwebs by the door and rustling some long-dead leaves that had collected in the corner. She could see better now. Her eyes scanned the shelves. Where was it? Could Gav have moved it? She took a step forward and something crunched beneath her shoe. She looked down and saw glass. Broken glass... and pebbles.

The jam jar had shattered into a thousand pieces as though hurled down with tremendous force. Pebbles and wilted water plants were strewn all over the floor. Freddie, the coffin and the sarcophagus had gone!

It was then she saw it. Or thought she did. A shape. Toad-like, but bigger, much bigger than a toad. Squatting among the flowerpots and seed trays at the back of the shed. Infinitely darker than the shadow around it. She caught the glint of a single fiery eye and stood transfixed. It seemed to her to be a portal into hell.

Suddenly it moved, scuttling crabwise, along the shelf. She let out a terrified shriek and blundered blindly out.

***

'It must have been the cat,' said Josh, when they had finally managed to calm her down. 'Gav must've left the door open when he put the mower away.'

But Katie wasn't sure. 'Perhaps it was about as big as a cat,' she conceded. 'But it didn't move like a cat. It moved in a funny way. Sort of sideways like a crab. And it had this red eye...and it just crouched there with this eye like a great big hunched up toad...' she shuddered at the memory.

'I don't know what you thought you saw,' said Andy, 'but it must've been a *person* who took Freddie. There's no sign of Dad's specs case or the trainers box. A cat couldn't have made off with that lot. It must've been a person that did it.'

'A little person,' said Josh, grinning. 'An evil little crabby, toady person.' And he hopped about the room, a crazed expression on his face.

'Maybe Dad did it,' suggested Katie. 'He wasn't very pleased about his handkerchief and the specs case.'

'No,' said Andy, 'Dad can be annoying at times but he wouldn't do that.'

'Well who then?' she asked. 'Who took Freddie?'

'Does it really matter?' yawned Josh. 'The subject's becoming a bore.'

'You were in the shed this afternoon,' said Andy.

Josh looked behind him, then placed a finger on his chest. 'Who me?'

'Yes, before Katie got home from swimming, you and Eddie Pomroy – smoking those cigarettes he pinched off his dad – I saw you.'

'Smoking!' shrieked Katie. 'You'll die!'

'Keep your voice down can't you, Mum'll hear. Anyway, I didn't inhale.'

'No, you were too busy choking from what I could hear,' said Andy.

'You won't do it again, will you Josh?' said Katie.

Her brother looked sheepish. 'No,' he said, 'I didn't like it anyway.'

'Only,' Katie continued, 'when we went to the Natural History Museum we saw this lung, well two actually, one was normal and one, the smoker's, was like a bit of old sponge, with great big holes and...'

Andy interrupted the biology lesson. 'Was everything okay in the shed when you went in?'

'What do you mean "was everything okay"?' said Josh. 'Of course it was.'

'Well it can't have been Gav's fault then, can it?'

'What are you on about?'

'Well, it can't have been him,' Andy went on, blissfully unaware of the dangerous glint in Josh's eye, 'because he only ever comes on Friday mornings and you said that everything was all right when you went in there in the afternoon.'

Josh's face had flushed a warning red. 'What are you trying to say?' he said slowly. 'Are you trying to say that *I* did it?'

'No, of course not. I'm just trying to pinpoint the time it happened. It couldn't have been before you were in there, so…'

'LOOK!' Josh shouted. 'I'M TELLING YOU THE TRUTH! WHEN I LEFT THAT SHED THE FISH WAS IN IT, RIGHT?'

He stormed out of the room, knocking over a chair as he went, and slamming the door. They could hear him banging about upstairs. Eventually his speakers went on at full blast.

'Well! What's the matter with him?' said Andy.

'He's got hormones,' said Katie, launching into more biology. 'All teenagers are like that because they've got hormones. They make you shout a lot and slam doors.'

'Dad must have them then,' said Andy thoughtfully.

'Oh no,' said Katie. 'Dad's much too old.'

Chapter 3

That night Josh couldn't sleep. He tossed and turned in bed trying to get comfortable but the moment he closed his eyes the sounds began again. Scratching, scuffling sounds, like mice behind the skirting or squirrels in the eaves. Sometimes they seemed so close that he could have sworn they came from something right beside his bed.

When he switched the light on to investigate, they always stopped. That made it all the more unnerving. He would sit bolt upright, listening intently, staring into space and he would hear… nothing. Not a thing. Just the usual night-time noises, the creaks and groans the house made as it settled down to rest, and sometimes the distant rattle of a slow goods-train or the barking of a dog.

He got up several times and looked around. Once, he knelt down and put his ear next to the skirting board but he couldn't hear anything. Another time, he peered nervously beneath the bed like he used to every night when he was four.

Of course, he knew he was getting things out of proportion. He was perfectly aware of that. But, in the middle of the night when you'd been trying to get to sleep for hours and you'd got problems on your mind, that was not at all surprising he told himself. He pulled the duvet over his head and resolved to blot things out and force himself to sleep.

But then there was the itching. He couldn't blot that out. His armpits were on fire with all the scratching he'd done. Perhaps it was that deodorant he'd pinched from Dad: *He-Man by Renoir*. It was supposed to make you irresistible to women but so far it hadn't had the slightest effect on Melissa.

He fell to musing on Melissa. She was one of his problems, or rather the lack of her was. Melissa, the best-looking girl in LV9. In the whole year. In the whole school even. He thought of the gleaming shoulder-length fair hair framing the perfect oval face, the big blue eyes and long dark lashes, the infectious sense of fun and ready smile. He really liked her. He had liked her for ages but he had never dared to so much as speak to her alone. The way things were, he thought, he never would.

A load of them were off to Stanton Springs next week to celebrate the end of term and Melissa would be there. But so would Michael Buss. And that was another problem. Michael Buss was an idiot with a big mouth and no depth of character. But quite a lot of girls seemed to like him. He hoped Melissa wasn't one of them.

He wished he was as tall as Michael Buss. He couldn't wait until he was fourteen like him. Maybe then he would shoot up in height as well.

If only he had the guts to ask her out. He was sure that she'd appreciate his great qualities once she got to know him. He wasn't bad looking and that zit on his nose had almost gone. Though it was true that there was another one about to erupt on his chin. If he could manage to ask her out between spots he might just have a chance…

The crash was like a thunderclap, so shocking was its suddenness. No more than a metre or so away from him something heavy had smashed onto the floor.

Josh sat up and fumbled for the switch on the bedside light. He sprang out of bed and what he saw made him gasp. There, stranded on its side, like a ship with a broken hull, lay his beautiful PlayStation. Its smart plastic casing was riven through with an enormous crack.

He felt sick as he looked at it. He picked it up and put it back up on his desk. But he knew it wouldn't work even before he plugged it in and tried to switch it on. It had fallen with such force that it had left a dent in the wooden floor.

But how could it have fallen off all by itself?

An unwelcome thought formed slowly in his brain: what if there was something *in* this room? Not in the roof or down behind the skirting. But here, now, *in this room*. And not a mouse but something bigger, a great deal bigger – it would have to be big to knock his PlayStation off the desk. A *rat,* maybe. A *huge* one. Hiding. Waiting until he went to sleep.

He went over to the door and flicked the switch beside it. The harsh glare of the ceiling light flooded everything, illuminating the dark corners, dispelling the shadows beneath his desk and by the curtains. Nervously he scanned his room. There was nowhere that a giant rat could hide. Nowhere except…the wardrobe door was open. Just a little. Had it been like that when he came in? He remembered what Katie had said about something in the shed and he felt his scalp prickle.

His cricket bat was propped against the wall. Slowly he closed his fingers around its handle and noiselessly drew it up, raising it shoulder-high. Behind him and unnoticed his bedside light flickered like a guttering candle and went out. He crept stealthily towards the wardrobe all the while listening intently like a wary cat. Then, taking a deep breath, he flung the door wide open.

The smell was what hit him first. A rotting smell like meat gone off. Perhaps something had crawled inside and died. He stood there, bat in hand, uncertain what to do. He didn't really want to look but he knew he wouldn't sleep until he had. He wondered if Dad would mind too much if he went and woke him up. He glanced at his watch: one-fifteen, perhaps he'd better not. He was just making up his mind to shut the wardrobe door and leave things until the morning, when there was a sudden scuffling and he knew that something very much alive had been disturbed.

Panic made him lash out blindly with his bat. Then the scuffling started up in earnest. Something was scuttling amongst the clutter on the wardrobe floor and then up the wall behind the screen of clothes. It sounded large. *Very* large. Its fetid smell, now quite strong, stung his nostrils. Fear and nausea rose up into his throat, almost choking him. He thought about making a dash for the door.

But, before he could take so much as a single retreating step, something stopped him. The hanging rail tipped out of its socket at one end and sweatshirts, trousers and hoodies slipped off their hangers and collapsed about his ears.

His mind was filled with a sudden, horrifying image. The rat, trapped perhaps amongst the clothing piled on top of him, might frantically scrabble to make its escape. It might scuttle perhaps down the back of his neck or across his shoulders, its greasy fur brushing his bare skin, its long, thin, hairless tail flicking against his cheek...

He plunged into a positive frenzy of terror. He tried to wrench the clothing off but it seemed to wrap itself around his head and throat. Gasping, he dropped the bat and staggered backwards, tearing at the coiling clothes that seemed now to be a single, living thing. It twisted itself around his chest, binding and tightening, squeezing the air out of his lungs, crushing his ribs until he felt sure that they would crack. In the end he couldn't even breathe, much less call for help. He was sure that he was going to die and then...

As abruptly as it had all begun, it stopped. The clothes released their grip and dropped away, flopping limply to the floor around his feet. He kicked them from him like something contaminated and lurched exhaustedly towards the door.

He never saw what it was that tripped him up. Something caught him around the ankle. Afterwards he supposed that it might have been the leg of his chair. But somehow it felt alive: a small, cold hand that seemed to grip and hold him fast. He staggered and then lost his balance, landing heavily, sideways, upon the wooden floor. Somewhere, high above him, there was a loud bang, like gunshot. Then everything went dark and he knew nothing more.

Chapter 4

'Andy,' said Katie, in her most confiding tone, 'I definitely think there's something wrong with Josh.'

'Tell me something I don't know.' Andy was by the dustbins trying to mend a puncture on his bike.

'Well?' she said. 'Aren't you going to ask me why?' She loitered expectantly but he appeared to be completely absorbed in what he was doing.

'You told me before.' He had plunged an inner tube into a bucket of water and was stooped over it watching for the bubbles to come up.

'No I didn't!' Katie was indignant.

'You said that he had hormones.'

'No, I didn't mean about that. I meant: don't you want to know what he's been doing?'

'Well, what?' Andy stood up and faced her, hands on hips. 'Tell me quickly and then go away. Can't you see I'm busy?'

Katie took exception to his tone. 'I'm *not* going to tell you now,' she said, 'unless you say sorry for being rude.'

'Fine, don't then.' Andy returned to his bucket.

She stood there for a moment watching him sulkily. But it was too much to keep all to herself.

'He's worn his hat all morning,' she said.

Andy gave her a withering look. 'So what?'

'His *woolly* hat!' she said, her voice rising to a squeak, 'his *beanie* one! He's got it pulled right down around his ears. He's been wearing it for hours. In all this heat. He must be sweltering.'

'Perhaps he likes it.'

She tried a different tack. 'And have you seen his room?'

Andy sighed. 'No, but I expect *you* have.'

'I couldn't help it could I? He left the door wide open. It's in the most horrendous mess.'

'So what's new?' said Andy. 'Now, if you've finished, I'd like to be left to get on with this. Ah! *There* it is!' He had found the puncture point and went over to fetch his repair kit from on top of the wall.

'No, really,' Katie insisted, 'you should see it. It's like a bomb's gone off.'

'Yeah, yeah,' said Andy.

'He's pulled his curtains down and one of the legs has come off his chair and he's torn all his posters off the wall and there's ripped up books all over the floor and his PlayStation's got a great big crack and...'

Andy stopped what he was doing. 'His PlayStation? Are you sure?'

At last she had his undivided attention.

'Go and see for yourself if you don't believe me,' she said triumphantly.

***

'This is serious.' Andy surveyed the wreckage of his brother's room. He picked his way through piles of clothes and bits of paper and cracked DVD cases. Katie followed.

'I told you,' she said.

'Be careful, there's some glass.' Andy bent down to have a look. It seemed to be the remains of a light bulb. He peered up at the ceiling rose – there was nothing but the metal bayonet cap hanging from it. 'Looks like it exploded.'

He poked around in the debris with his foot and half uncovered something that made him start. He quickly toed a T-shirt over it before Katie had a chance to see.

'Do you think Mum and Dad will understand about Josh's hormones?' said Katie. 'Or do you think that they'll be cross?'

'I think that they'll be cross,' said Andy.

***

They found Josh on the computer in the sitting room. He was staring intently at the monitor and didn't even glance up when they came in.

'He doesn't look well does he?' whispered Katie. He had dark circles around his eyes and his face was pale beneath the beanie cap. He was scrolling through a search page on the Web. The two moved closer in to have a look.

Spook the **Spooks.** Banish **paranormal** pests
Step by step guide on DVD. Half price £15.95...
www.**spook**a**spook**.co.uk/

Ghosts, Ghouls, Gremlins, other unwelcome visitors..
Elimination of **ghosts, poltergeists**, apparitions, etc.
An **Exorcism** for Every Occasion; by Wraith, Harold R.N.,
www.doctorwraith-removals.com/

'What are you looking at those for?' said Andy.

Josh's eyes stayed fixed upon the screen. 'None of your business.'

'Well, your room's going to be everybody's business when Mum and Dad get home.'

'My room?' said Josh. 'What about my room? Have you been spying through the keyhole?'

'No need,' said Andy. 'You left the door wide open.'

'But I locked it!' He fumbled in his pocket. 'Here's the key!'

'Well it's open now.'

'Why did you break all those things?' said Katie, 'your beautiful PlayStation…?'

'I didn't! I didn't break any of them!'

'Well who did then?'

'I don't know.' His voice had a defeated ring. 'That's just it, I just don't know.'

'You *must* know,' insisted Andy. 'It's *your* room.'

'But I don't.' He turned and looked his brother squarely in the face. His skin had a greyish tinge. He really did look ill.

'If I tell you something, will you promise not to take the mickey?'

'Depends.'

'On what?'

'On whether it's the truth or not.'

'Last night I couldn't sleep,' said Josh. 'I kept hearing these sounds.'

'What sounds?' said Katie, saucer-eyed.

'A sort of scuffling – I dunno.'

'Mice?' suggested Andy.

'Then, while I lay there, suddenly there was this almighty crash and when I put the light on there was my PlayStation – on the floor, completely wrecked.'

'Was it on the edge?' said Andy.

'Nowhere near.'

'Weird.'

'What's even weirder – no one else heard a thing. I kept expecting Dad to storm in any minute.'

'Yeah, that *is* weird, I agree,' said Andy.

'Yeah, well, the PlayStation really freaked me out. And then I got the idea that there was something in the wardrobe – a rat I thought it might be – so I got my bat and went for it.'

'Did you get it?'

'No. It got me.'

'The rat got you?'

'It was no rat. It could do things, it had powers – it collapsed the hanging rail and tipped a load of clothes on top of me.'

'Oh yeah, major powers,' mocked Andy.

'You don't understand – those clothes...they were alive! They tried to smother me!'

'Of course they did,' said Andy, 'and then when they'd done that they went and trashed your room. You'll have to think up a better story than that by the time Mum and Dad get home.'

'It's true!' said Josh. 'Something tripped me up and I fell and then I must have passed out or gone to sleep or… I dunno … but in the morning, when I woke up, the room was … it was…' His voice faltered.

'In a great big mess?' offered Katie. She sounded sorry for him.

'Do you expect us to believe you slept through all of that and you never heard a thing?' said Andy.

'I don't care what you believe but that's what happened.'

Out of the blue, Katie suddenly said: 'Why are you wearing that hat?'

This seemed to be the final straw. Josh's face crumpled. Tears welled up.

Slowly he peeled the beanie off his head to reveal hair that, apart from its colour, looked rather like a very close-mown lawn.

'You're bald!' Katie was appalled.

'How did you do it?' said Andy.

'Eddie borrowed some clippers off his mum.'

'You mean he pinched them off her.' Mrs Pomroy was a hairdresser and Eddie always got his haircuts free.

'I wanted a *Number Eight* like his,' said Josh.

'But you got a *Number Nought* instead.'

'I set it on eight, I know I did, but the lever must've moved – or something moved it – and I shaved this strip right through the middle. So I had to even it up all round didn't I? And it ended up like this.'

'Mum and Dad'll have a fit,' said Katie.

'Talking of Mum and Dad,' said Andy, 'wouldn't it be a good idea to try and clear things up a bit?'

But the other two weren't listening. Their eyes were fixed on an object floating in mid air about two metres away. A bowl of fruit had levitated off the sideboard and three oranges and a banana, hovering in perfect formation like a fleet of flying saucers, took aim and hurled themselves at Josh.

Chapter 5

Josh managed to duck only just in time. The fruit, travelling at tremendous speed, missed him by barely centimetres, splattering against the opposite wall and leaving sticky trails as it slid towards the floor. In next to no time reinforcements were lining up: three apples, an overripe plum and a rather wrinkly peach. The latter two didn't appear to pose much of a threat, but the apples, being of the hard, green variety, looked distinctly dangerous.

The children dived for cover behind the sofa. Milliseconds later the missiles whizzed head-high over them and smashed against the wall behind them, followed closely by the empty bowl which also shattered, showering them with bits of pottery.

Then everything went quiet. Cautiously Andy peered around an arm of the sofa and eyed the open door. 'Let's make a run for it!'

But Katie vigorously shook her head.

'You two go,' urged Josh. 'Go on! You'll be all right. Go!'

Still Katie wouldn't budge.

'It's me they're after – watch!' Josh raised his pale face above the parapet of the sofa-back. A sudden gust of wind rushed into the airless room, billowing out the curtains and lifting the paper from the printer. The pages swirled around his head swooping and diving like mobbing seagulls. They became more and more insistent, battering his face and neck. He tried to beat them off, his arms flailing wildly and with anguished little gasps he made a desperate dash for the door.

'JOSH DON'T!' It was Andy's voice – but too late. Just as he reached it, the door slammed violently in his face. In the corner the bookcase rocked then toppled forwards coming to rest in mid-fall against a chair. Hardbound volumes, paperbacks and magazines all tumbled towards him in a landslide. A heavy-looking tome seemed to aim for his head. It dealt him a glancing blow and he fell, apparently senseless, to the floor.

'He's dead!' shrieked Katie, flinging herself onto her knees beside his lifeless form.

But in a moment he had rolled over onto his side and opened his eyes. He rubbed an angry red lump that was starting to appear on his forehead. There was a paper-cut on his cheek. 'Ow, my head hurts.'

'I'm not surprised.' Andy had bent down to pick up the offending book. 'This thing weighs a ton.'

The book looked familiar. It was the one that Katie had used when making the sarcophagus for Freddie. And unless he was mistaken, it seemed to have fallen open at the very page from which she had been copying.

'You ought to have a cold thingy on that bump,' said Katie, who had high hopes of getting her First Aid Badge in the not-too-distant future. 'Or maybe I should put you in the whatchamacallit position – do you feel sick at all?'

Josh scowled and rubbed his head.

'You just stay on your side like that and bend this leg like that,' she went on. 'And then you bring your arm over your chest like *this* – or maybe it's like *that* – and your chin…'

'Ouch! Gerroff me will you!' Josh, wrenched himself free from Katie's grip and struggled up. 'I've bloody well had enough of this – I've bloody well had enough!' He kicked out angrily at a book that was in his way and flung out of the room and up the stairs.

'Well, don't blame me if you drop down dead then,' Katie called after his disappearing back. 'You're supposed to stay still until the ambulance arrives. And you should be watched.'

'So should you,' muttered Josh, 'by men in white coats.' And he sluiced his sore head under the cold-water tap in the bathroom.

Downstairs, Andy was deep in thought. In fact he was more than thoughtful – his brain was positively itching with ideas. Fantastic, incredible, unbelievable ideas. But then, after what had just gone on, nothing was too impossible to believe.

'…Well, *don't* you?' Someone was trying to break into his reverie. A small, but insistent voice was badgering him. As usual, it turned out to belong to Katie.

'What did you say?'

She gave an exasperated sigh. 'I *said*: don't you think that Josh should be lying down?'

He stared at her, puzzled.

'Brown Owl says that after an accident the patient should be kept calm and comfortable and then you ought to call a doctor.'

'He's not a patient and he looks perfectly all right to me. When Mum and Dad get back we'll tell them and they can decide.'

'Tell them!' she exclaimed. 'How can we tell them? Books and fruit flying about all on their own – they'll never believe it!'

She had a point. He hardly believed it himself and he had seen it with his own two eyes.

'Well, we'll make something up then – an accident. Anyway, they'll soon be home.'

Katie pouted and gave a deep shrug. Overruled again. 'Well *I* don't think he looks all right. *I* think he looks *awful*. There's definitely something wrong with him.'

'Yes,' conceded Andy. 'And,' he added, talking more to himself than to Katie, 'I think I might know what.'

Katie perked up. 'What?'

'It's only a theory – I've got to check it out.'

'What is it?'

'You'll see.' And he made for the door.

'Where are you going?'

'To his room to have a look.'

'I'll come with you then.'

'No,' said Andy, 'this might upset you.'

'I'm not staying down here all by myself, I'm coming with you.'

'Well, don't say I didn't warn you.'

***

Andy carefully laid the open book beside the T-shirt on the floor while Katie watched him from the doorway. They could hear the sound of running water in the bathroom. Josh seemed to be having a shower. So much the better, Andy thought, no interruptions.

'You wait there and tell me if he comes.'

'Must I?' said Katie, 'I want to see what you're doing.'

'I'll only be a minute.'

He knelt down with his back towards her, obscuring her view, and gently lifted off the T-shirt and cast it to one side.

The moment he saw it again he knew that he was right. He picked it up and examined it. The symbols, down to their smallest detail, were identical to the ones in the book. Even the colours were a perfect match. And if they looked the same why couldn't they mean the same? It stood to reason that they could. After all, hadn't they been used for thousands of years, time and time again?

For a brief moment he revelled in his cleverness. This was the cause of what was wrong with Josh! This was the key to it all! But then it dawned on him. It was one thing finding out the cause. It was quite another knowing how to put a stop to it. That would require an expert. And where was he to find one of those?

It was too late before he heard her coming up behind him. She gave a little gasp and he half turned to face her. Katie was staring, eyes round with shock, transfixed by what she saw in his hands. It was Freddie's sarcophagus.

Chapter 6

'It wasn't exactly a lie,' said Josh. 'I was just a bit economical with the truth that's all.' He was sitting on the topmost stair, the picture of misery, dripping wet and huddled in a towel.

'It *was* a lie,' insisted Katie. 'We found Freddie's sarcophagus in your room.'

'Yes, but that's all you found.'

'You're splitting hairs,' said Andy. 'The point is you said you hadn't taken it and you had.'

'No,' said Josh, 'I never mentioned the box. All I said was that I never took the fish – and I didn't. I just emptied everything out of the trainers box and left it all on the shelf in the shed. That's the truth – take it or leave it.'

'Well, where's Freddie *now*, then?'

'I don't know,' he said wearily. 'And to be honest, Katie, I don't care either. I mean I'm sorry I did it and everything – took the box I mean – but right now I've got more important things on my mind.'

They didn't need to ask what things. It was obvious that he was thinking about this morning. They all were. Had they really seen it? Books and fruit and pieces of paper flying around of their own accord! It would be so much nicer to think that they hadn't. So much more comfortable to return to the ordinary problems of everyday life. Like school and friends and pocket money. But no one said as much. Instead they agreed to meet again downstairs in five minutes as soon as Josh was dressed '...because,' said Andy, 'I've got something important to talk to you about and it won't wait.'

Five minutes later Josh had locked himself in the most private and convenient room in the house, where no one and nothing could get at him. He put the seat-cover down and sat staring sullenly at the floor, feeling resentful and depressed. Why was all this happening to him? Why didn't the others seem to care at all? Why were they more bothered about his taking a stupid shoebox that had been his in the first place anyway?

Well, he decided, if they wanted to speak to him it was just too bad. He didn't want to speak to *them*. He reached up to the narrow window ledge behind him and grabbed a battered copy of *Goal Fever*. Flicking through its pages he turned to one at random and began to read. He read the opening sentence five times. But it was no good, he couldn't concentrate. All he could think about was the ghost and how he could get rid of it.

That it *was* a ghost he was convinced. It was probably a poltergeist. He'd read about them on the Net. They were prone to throwing things and slamming doors, exploding light bulbs and the like. Of course there was one difference: it seemed that poltergeists were noisy things and his one wasn't — at least not all the time. But otherwise the theory seemed to fit quite well. But as for getting rid of it, well, that was another matter...

A sudden knocking on the door interrupted his thoughts. 'How much longer are you going to be in there?' It was Andy's voice. 'We've been waiting ages!' He sounded cross.

Josh looked up and was just about to reply that he was going to stay there as long as he felt like staying there, when he noticed something on the door. Something he felt sure had not been there when he had come in just now and locked it. Writing. The strange spiky script looked as though it had been put on with a fine brush dipped in red paint. It said: *The Eye of Ra is watching you.*

He didn't stop to read it twice.

***

'Why are you saying that it's not a ghost?' demanded Josh. The three were sitting round the kitchen table discussing the events of the morning and the night before. 'It's got to be a ghost. You saw the things it did.'

Katie nodded energetically.

'Yes,' said Andy, 'but it's not.'

'It's obviously a ghost,' Josh insisted. 'It says about them on the Net – it's what they call a poltergeist. If it isn't a ghost, what is it, then? Or are we all hallucinating?'

'What's that?' enquired Katie, always keen to increase her vocabulary.

'He means: are we imagining it?' Andy explained. 'No, we're not. But it isn't a ghost – at least not the usual kind.'

'Usual! What's usual about ghosts?'

'Well, what I mean is: you can't exorcise it in the usual way, I shouldn't think.'

'Exercise it?' piped Katie, struggling to keep up with the finer points of the conversation. 'Like jogging, d'you mean?'

Andy sighed, 'Ex*or*cise not ex*erc*ise – it's a ritual.'

31

Katie looked blank.

'A *ceremony*...for getting rid of a ghost.'

'Okay, know-all,' said Josh, 'tell us what it is then.'

'That's simple,' said Andy. 'It's a curse.'

There was a moment of silent disbelief and then Josh said: 'Are you seriously saying that someone's gone and cursed me?'

'Well, not exactly. You sort of brought it on yourself.'

'Huh?'

'When you took Freddie's sarcophagus you sort of set it off. You see...it's an ancient Egyptian curse.'

Josh stared at him. 'Have you gone nuts? That's even crazier than ghosts.'

'It might seem crazy, but I'm sure it's right.'

Andy bent down and heaved a large volume onto the kitchen table. 'This book,' he said, 'is the one that Katie used when she was making Freddie's sarcophagus.'

'So?'

'So this:' said Andy, 'Katie made a perfect job of it. She copied it beautifully. All the pictures and the hieroglyphics – even the colours – are identical to the ones on this page here.'

Katie preened. 'Yes, I was very, very pleased with myself because I did it exactly like the ones on the coffin in the book.'

'But,' continued Andy, 'what Katie didn't know – because she hadn't bothered to read the opposite page – was that what she had copied was a curse, a curse that the ancient Egyptians used to protect their tombs from robbers. It says all about it here.' And he began to read aloud: *'The ancient Egyptians went to extraordinary lengths to protect their mummies. They built false doors and hidden corridors and secret chambers in their tombs to fool the robbers. But despite all these elaborate precautions thefts continued to take place. So as a last resort it was not unknown for curses to be used. The one shown here is of a particularly virulent kind. It could only be removed (for all spells had to have an antidote in case of accident) by a secret ritual involving charms and various magical paraphernalia.'*

'Let me see that.' Josh pulled the book towards him and examined it intently. Then he compared it with Freddie's box. He took a while, looking from the book to the box and the box to the book several times. At last, he said grudgingly: 'You could be right I s'pose. But it seems a bit far-fetched.'

'Well, it's the only thing that fits,' said Andy. 'And it does fit perfectly, you must admit. When Katie put Freddie into the box all bandaged up like a mummy – that somehow or other activated the curse. Then you came along and took the box away and, well, we know what happened.' He folded his arms with a triumphant air, 'Good theory, huh?'

But Josh wasn't feeling in the mood for handing out congratulations. He frowned into the middle distance, nibbling the fingernails of one hand and scratching absent-mindedly at an armpit with the other.

'It's a catastrophe.' He gave a sigh of deepest gloom. 'I'm doomed.'

'What's a…a catass…?' Katie faltered. 'What does that mean?' she said.

'It means,' Josh flared at her, 'that you're an annoying waste of space and that it's all your fault!'

'I don't see how you can say that!' said Katie. 'If you hadn't taken Freddie's box…'

'And if you hadn't got Mum to make me give it to you in the first place…'

'Does it matter whose fault it was, anyway?' said Andy. 'What matters is what we do about it now.' He had this calm, logical way of talking sometimes that made him seem older than eleven.

'Yeah…well…what do you suggest?' said Josh. 'An ancient Egyptian exorcism?'

'Funny you should say that,' said Andy, 'because I've had an idea.' He closed the book with a heavy thud. On the front of the dust jacket was a picture of the usual ancient-Egyptian-type ladies, all in profile, walking sideways. Next to them a mummy was lying on a sort of table that had legs like lion's legs and paws for feet. Below the title was a name: *Lobelia Carter-Smythe.* 'We've got to get in touch with her.'

'Get in touch with *her*? What are you on about *"get in touch with her"*?' The idea was ridiculous.

'Well, it says in the book that there's always an antidote.'

'So?'

'So, if she knows about the curse, it stands to reason that she just might know about the antidote, that's all.'

Josh said nothing. But inside him a tiny flame of hope ignited.

'It's worth a try,' said Andy.

'Maybe,' said Josh. A note of cautious optimism had crept into his tone. 'But how are we going to find her? She won't be in the Yellow Pages.'

'Well, it says here…' Andy turned to the inside of the dust jacket and proceeded to read: '*Dame Lobelia Carter-Smythe CBE has travelled extensively in Egypt for over thirty years. She has written more than twenty books and*

34

is a world-authority on the ancient Egyptian way of death. When not excavating in the Valley of the Kings she lives in Little Deddbury in Buckinghamshire. – That's that little village near Amersham where Auntie Alice lives. You just go to the end of the Metropolitan line and take a bus – it's easy.'

Josh had brightened up considerably. 'It isn't a big place, we could ask at the post office or the church or somewhere like that – they might know.'

'Bound to,' said Andy. 'Now let's get on and tidy up before Mum and Dad get back.'

Chapter 7

'There are no Dames in this telephone directory,' said Katie. 'I've looked and looked.'

'You should've been looking under *"C"* not *"D"*,' said Josh. 'And anyway that's the wrong directory, we haven't got the one for Deddbury.'

'I tried Directory Enquiries,' said Andy, 'but they couldn't give me her telephone number unless I could give them her address – so that was hopeless.'

'Well, I give up,' said Josh. He had been trawling the Internet for almost an hour and apart from a long list of all her books (most of which now seemed to be out of print) he had found barely a mention of her name. 'She must be dead I reckon. So that's that.'

'What is a Dame, anyway?' enquired Katie. 'Are dames important people?'

'Dunno,' said Andy. 'I suppose so.'

'Maybe dames are too important to be put in the ordinary telephone directory,' said Katie. 'Like the Queen. Maybe they've got a special directory all to themselves.'

The three sat down despondently at the kitchen table. Tracing the whereabouts of Dame Lobelia Carter-Smythe was proving to be a difficult task. They had quickly agreed that the original idea of simply going to the village and asking people about her would not be practical. Supposing she had moved, or gone away? Or supposing, when they turned up on her doorstep, she refused to help them, or worse, complained to their parents that they had been making a nuisance of themselves? No, it would be much the best plan, they decided, to break the ice by telephoning first. But how to find her number? That was the problem. And it was proving to be a problem that they couldn't seem to solve.

They settled down to eat the sandwiches Mum had left for them in the fridge. Mrs Ridley had just telephoned to say that they had been delayed at the shopping centre. Browsing through wallpaper and curtain material had taken longer than expected and they'd only now got around to looking at furniture for the dining room.

'It's a pity they're not doing up the sitting-room,' said Andy. 'I couldn't get those fruit stains off the wall, the juice has soaked into the paper and it's all torn and dented where the bowl smashed into it.'

Josh looked alarmed. Damage in his bedroom was one thing – apart from a few missing curtain-hooks, there was nothing much a grown-up would notice now that he had stashed his PlayStation discreetly out of sight, Superglued the broken leg back on the chair and replaced the light bulb. But anything amiss in his father's territory would immediately be pounced upon. Dad was sure to be in a filthy mood after a day spent traipsing round *Shoppers' Paradise*. Josh knew from bitter experience that, as the oldest, if there was any blame to be dished out he would be the one to get served first.

'Isn't there some way we could cover it up?' he asked. 'Couldn't we stick the bookcase there or something?'

'That would just draw attention to it,' said Andy. 'Dad would want to know why we'd been moving things.'

'We could put a picture up,' suggested Katie. 'I did a beautiful one of *Elephas Maximus*. That's Latin. It's a sort of elephant. We did it for our endangered wildlife project and Mrs. Turner said mine was the best. It's on the wall next to my bed but you can have it if you like.'

A deafening silence greeted this generous offer.

'Well?' persisted Katie, 'Shall I go and get it then?'

'No,' said Josh.

'The thing is, Katie,' said Andy, 'I don't think we could go sticking up your picture either. It would have the same effect as putting the bookcase there, as far as Dad's concerned.'

'And anyway,' said Josh, 'I'd rather look at fruit stains.'

'Very funny,' said Katie. 'Ha, ha.'

At any other time this promising exchange might well have been the prelude to an enjoyable battle of words. But Josh didn't have the heart to follow through with any more sarcastic barbs and even Katie wasn't really in the mood. Andy seemed preoccupied. Something threatening and unpredictable was keeping them on edge. They felt exhausted and oppressed by constant watchfulness. They knew the curse would strike again. But they didn't know how or where or when.

They ate in a pensive silence that was broken only by the sound of their own chewing and occasional slurping of orange juice or cola. Suddenly Andy, who had raised his sandwich to his mouth and was about to take another bite, slammed it back down on his plate and let out a triumphant cry. 'Of course!'

The others almost jumped out of their skins. *'What?'*

'Katie's absolutely right!'

Katie brightened up. 'Do you want me to go and get it now then?'

For a moment he was baffled. 'What?'

'My picture – shall I go and get it?'

Josh gave a barely suppressed groan.

'No, not that,' said Andy, smiling. 'You were right about the other thing – about important people having a directory all to themselves – they do – there *is* a book!'

***

The reference part of the library had a special feel about it, different from the rest of the building. Its atmosphere was hushed and reverential and the books on its shelves looked drab compared with the colourful rows downstairs. There were four long tables at which a handful of people sat making notes or deeply immersed in weighty volumes. The children, feeling a little like intruders in a church, trooped across the polished floor towards the bookshelves at the far end.

An elderly woman with steel-rimmed spectacles and a beaky nose looked up as they passed – disapprovingly, Katie thought.

Katie fingered her necklace self-consciously. It was her special one. She had made it herself from beads she had collected over months and months. Some she had found lying loose in a drawer, the remains of one of Mum's bits of jewellery. The rest she'd got from the arts and crafts shop in the High Street and by doing swaps at school. She had started off a fad amongst her friends. It quickly spread to the rest of the girls in the class. Soon there was a positive frenzy of bead threading and swapping throughout the junior school. The Head had banned it in the end when one of the boys had stuck a large bead up his nostril for a laugh and had to be taken to hospital to get it out. So now she could only wear them after school or at weekends or in the holidays.

Perhaps she hadn't threaded them strongly enough, or perhaps she pulled a little too hard, but the string suddenly snapped and the whole lot went scattering all over the floor.

Peace was instantly dispelled. Beads rolled everywhere, under tables and chairs and people's feet. Katie, her face a ripe tomato red, immediately sank down on all fours and tried to pick them up. Soon everyone was pitching in – even the stern old lady – and handing them back to her with friendly smiles.

Josh kept aloof from this embarrassment, retiring to a corner and suddenly becoming deeply engrossed in volume 2 of the *Dictionary of Famous Sayings and Witty Aphorisms*. But Andy had genuinely not noticed. With his usual single-mindedness he had homed in on what they had come for. Next to the encyclopaedias and just below a copy of *Olde Moore's Almanac* he had spotted a thick, official-looking volume bound in red. It was an elderly edition of *Who's Who*.

Chapter 8

The entry in *Who's Who* was not a long one. It gave, rather ungallantly perhaps, Dame Lobelia's date of birth (way back in the distant mists of time) and a brief account of her education and career. Last, but by no means least as far as the children were concerned, came full details of her address and telephone number.

As it turned out Dame Lobelia no longer lived in Little Deddbury. The children could hardly believe their luck, however, when they discovered where she did live. No trains or buses were required to get to her, their own two feet would take them there in less than fifteen minutes – five minutes if they took their bikes. In fact, if they made what would be only a minor detour on their way home from the library they would pass her very door!

The idea seemed extremely tempting and they discussed the merits of doing just that as they set off homewards. Of course, they saw at once there was a snag: the library's *Who's Who* was not a new one. There was always the chance that she had moved again. But, as Andy pointed out, it was a lot newer than the information on the dust-jacket of her book, so at the very least it was worth a try wasn't it? What would be the harm, he said, in simply going there to have a look?

It took a little longer to find than they had thought it would. They had walked right around Willow Crescent and over Walnut Hill before they'd realised that they'd taken a wrong turn and had to stop and ask directions from a lady with a dog. Retracing their steps they made their way down Poppy Lane and Oak Tree Drive, turned second right and suddenly were there.

Apricot Grove was just an ordinary street full of ordinary semi-detached houses and number 24 was no different from the rest. True, it was unusual, perhaps, in having a neat front garden instead of just a square of concrete with a car on top. But otherwise, it looked completely nondescript. Until you looked again...

It was then you might just notice that the knocker on the door was not the typical run-of-the-mill affair. It was a grotesque human face. It had a lion's ears and mane and from its obscenely gaping mouth protruded a thick, red tongue. It must have given many an unwary visitor on a dark winter's afternoon a very nasty fright.

Then, if you happened to venture down the path a little way, you might observe, half hidden by the purple clematis beside the porch, a curious little statue. Nothing unusual in that perhaps – they had a garden gnome next door – but this one was a hippopotamus. And it was standing upright like a person – on lion's paws – and wearing a whole crocodile down its back.

And if you stepped into the porch and paused a moment to look up you might well spot, high above the lintel of the door, not a lucky horseshoe but a little T-shaped object with a loop on top. And next to that, a sort of pillar crossed with four bars.

42

They did, of course, venture down the path, something drew them on. The garden gate swung loosely on its hinges and seemed to be inviting them in. They noticed as they went through that the latch was quite distinctive. Not the anonymous sort to be found on other gates, this one looked like a creature. A human-headed mixture of a griffin and a sphinx, with a long snake-like tail.

They loitered by the doorway wondering what to do. They wondered if they dare now try the knocker. And, if they dared and if she answered it, they wondered what exactly they would say to her. Now that it had come to the crunch at last they were a little nervous.

They had a brief debate about it and had just resolved to go back home again and try to telephone when someone unlatched the gate. A small, broad, energetic woman, pulling in her wake a tartan shopping trolley, was coming down the path towards them. It was the stern old lady with the beaky nose who had helped Katie pick up her beads in the library.

Their first impulse was to leave immediately. But her considerable bulk stood between them and the exit to the street. Josh was searching desperately in his mind for some believable excuse for their presence in her front garden when she boomed good-naturedly at them: 'Ah! So you've come at last! I've been expecting you.'

They gazed at her in dumb astonishment. How could she have been expecting them?

'Well,' she said, moving briskly past them to the porch, 'you'd better come in'. She put her key in the lock and opened the front door.

The children shuffled uncertainly.

'*Well, come in then!* Don't loiter there, you're in the way – Bastet wants her tea.'

A sleek black cat threaded its way through the forest of their legs and over the threshold into the hall. The old lady motioned them forward with quick, impatient gestures of her hand and pointed at a couple of black plastic sacks, full to bursting and tied up with string.

'They've been here under my feet for almost a fortnight now,' she complained. 'I do think you could have come for them sooner. The others said someone would be back within the week. Still, you're here now I suppose... so better late than never.'

The children didn't move or speak. They simply stood there looking awkward.

'I'm sorry I can't help – my back you know. Where's the driver anyway, I didn't see the van just now?'

At last Josh found his voice. He cleared his throat nervously. 'I think that you've mistaken us for someone else.'

'Someone else? You *are* from the Scouts Association, are you not, come to collect the jumble for the fair?'

'No.'

'Well, who are you then? And what are you doing in my house?'

'You *told* us to come in,' said Katie.

The old lady narrowed her eyes. 'Haven't I seen you somewhere before?'

'Yes,' said Katie, 'in the library.'

'That's right!' She peered at Katie down her great hawk's nose. 'You were the child who dropped the beads.'

'Yes,' said Katie. 'Thank you for helping me to pick them up.'

'No need to thank me twice, young lady. As I recall you thanked me before and very politely too.'

44

Katie beamed.

'Well, I'm sorry that you're not here for the jumble, I must say, but perhaps now you'll be good enough to tell me what you want?'

The others looked at Josh. He hesitated. It was difficult to know how to begin. There was an awkward silence that seemed to go on and on. In the end he said: 'We've got your book – Mysterious Mummies...' And as an afterthought he added: 'You *are* Dame Lobelia Carter-Smythe aren't you?'

'You have my book?' She seemed delighted. 'How very gratifying! In its day it was a best seller of its kind, you know. But now it's out of print.' She sighed. 'I fear my views are too controversial for the powers that be. Still, no matter...have you got a pen?'

He looked confused.

'A pen...' she repeated, '...to sign my book...you do want me to autograph it don't you?'

'Oh no,' said Josh. 'That is, yes, we do, of course, but that's not why we're here.'

There was another pause and then he threw caution to the wind. 'The curse – the one that's in the book – it's on me!' he blurted out. 'Things have been happening to me – bad things – since yesterday when I took the sarcophagus and we thought that...that since it says that there's an antidote that you might be able to help us... perhaps...' He broke off, suddenly feeling foolish.

Dame Lobelia stared at him intently, her finger pressed against pursed lips. Finally she said: 'I think a cup of tea would be in order. I've got some scones and chocolate biscuits in the pantry. Do you like Victoria sponge?'

45

The children could only mumble and faintly nod their heads.

'Excellent. I made one yesterday. But first things first: do you wish to use the telephone to inform your parents of your whereabouts? Or perhaps you have one of those mobile contraptions that everybody seems to carry about these days?'

Josh shook his head. 'I lost mine.'

'So did I,' said Andy.

'They lost two *each*,' said Katie. 'So Dad won't let them have one anymore.'

'No loss at all in my opinion,' said Dame Lobelia. 'I manage perfectly well without one. They're a menace to peace and quiet in my view – people constantly shouting into them in public places and all those irritating ringtones.'

'We did leave a note though,' said Josh, 'saying we'd be at the library.'

'I see,' said Dame Lobelia. 'Well, that will have to do. Now tell me: would I be right in thinking that your parents don't know about your problem?'

She's a sharp old thing, thought Josh. 'I don't think that they'd exactly understand,' he said.

'Quite,' said Dame Lobelia, 'just as I thought. I am by no means unfamiliar with this attitude myself – even from colleagues. There is so much wilful ignorance about matters of the occult, I'm afraid.' She sighed. 'Well, it's only a white lie, I suppose, just to stop your parents worrying. Now, shall we all go through and have some tea?'

Chapter 9

Dame Lobelia's sitting room was a cross between a cosy, country cottage and a small, untidy museum. Flowery chintz curtains hung at the windows and comfy armchairs with overstuffed cushions were arranged around an old-fashioned, tiled fireplace. There were fire irons on the hearth.

All sorts of objects were stacked in corners and under side tables and piled on shelves. There was a foot from a broken statue. There were fragments of stone with hieroglyphic writing on them. There was a little alabaster box decorated with lotus flowers. Several large clay jars with curved bases lay upon their sides. And there were books everywhere.

An upright piano stood against one wall with a great number of faded photographs in frames grouped along the top. Josh went over to have a look. There were photos of Dame Lobelia in Egypt, excavating, trowel in hand, wearing long khaki outfits and wide-brimmed hats with veils to keep the flies away. There was a very small Dame Lobelia standing in front of a very large pyramid. There was Dame Lobelia shaking hands with important, official-looking people. Dame Lobelia sitting on a camel peering out across the desert, one hand capped above her eyes to shade them from the sun. Dame Lobelia in shorts…in *shorts?* Josh looked again, more closely this time – yes, definitely in shorts – though they were extremely long ones, it was true.

Against another wall stood a small, glass-fronted cabinet. Inside were not the usual china knick-knacks, but mementoes of Dame Lobelia's time in Egypt. Bits of pots, bowls with great cracks and holes in them, little figurines of cats with rings through their ears and noses and a rather frightening statuette of a woman with a lioness's head. She wore a great disc-shaped headdress with a rearing cobra-snake in front of it. Josh couldn't drag his eyes away from her. She fascinated and repelled him.

'Ah! I see you like my Sekhmet!' exclaimed Dame Lobelia, following his gaze. 'Isn't she delicious?'

'Delicious' was not the word he would have used.

'I dug her up during my third season at Thebes. The Egyptian Department of Antiquities was so delighted with my discoveries that they presented her to me as a gift.'

'She looks scary,' said Katie.

'Yes, she's really quite ferocious.' The old lady went over to the cabinet and took out the statuette. 'Her name means *Powerful One*,' she said gazing at it fondly. 'Sometimes she's called the *Eye of Ra* because she sees all and is there to wreak revenge upon humanity.'

Her last few words did not go down at all well with Josh. He went extremely pale and sat down very suddenly because his legs felt rather strange.

'What is it?' said Dame Lobelia. 'You look as if you've seen a ghost.'

It was left to Andy to explain about the writing on the toilet door. As Dame Lobelia listened her expression changed. 'I think you'd better tell me the rest,' she said sombrely. She sat down and passed around cups of tea and plates of cake and biscuits. 'Begin at the beginning and take care to leave nothing out.'

Katie began since it was Katie who had begun it all, so to speak. Then Josh told his part and Andy chipped in here and there with his. When they were done Dame Lobelia sat quietly for a while staring thoughtfully at the carpet and tapping her fingertips on the arm of her chair. At length she sighed deeply and said: 'I blame myself. I never should have put a photograph of that accursed coffin in my book.'

'But can you help us?' said Josh. 'Is there an antidote?'

'There is an antidote but I don't have it – at least not all of it.'

'But can you get it? Is it in a book somewhere?'

'It isn't as simple as that, I'm afraid.' She leaned back in her armchair and took a deep breath. 'You've told me your story and now I think it's time to tell you mine.' She gazed past them, through the window, at the quiet suburban street.

'Many, many years ago, when I was a green, young archaeologist, just starting out and ambitious to make a name for myself, I was excavating near the Valley of the Kings.'

'What's *excavating*?' said Katie, revived by the refreshments. 'And please may I have another piece of cake?'

'Certainly you may,' smiled Dame Lobelia. 'I see you have a healthy appetite – for words as well as cake. *Excavating* means digging for things, especially *ancient* things you know.

'Well, as I was saying, I was excavating near the Valley of the Kings. It was a remote and empty tomb and

49

there was nothing much of interest in it – only bits of broken pottery and fragments of sarcophagi. Tomb robbers had got there before me.' She chuckled. 'Thousands of years before me, to be precise.

'One day, however, when we were clearing rubble from a side-chamber we came across a secret door. It was made of stone and looked no different from the rest of the wall, so I never would have spotted it had it not been for the scorpion that came scuttling out from underneath. There was a tiny gap, you see, between the bottom of the door and the floor. One of my workmen was stung...'

'Did he die?' asked Josh.

'No, but he was extremely ill,' said Dame Lobelia. 'That was my first warning. I should have heeded it. I should have stopped the excavations there and then. But...' she sighed regretfully, 'being young and headstrong I went on. When we removed the door we found another chamber, but this one wasn't empty.'

She paused to pour a second cup of tea.

'Was there treasure in it?' asked Andy.

'Yes, but not the kind you're thinking of. There was just a perfectly preserved sarcophagus and inside that a coffin, beautifully decorated – the ones in the book in fact – and inside that...'

'A mummy!' cried Katie, clapping her hands excitedly. 'Inside the coffin was a mummy with a beautiful golden mask, wasn't there?'

'No,' said Dame Lobelia. 'The mummy had been stolen long ago. Snatched by robbers looking for precious ornaments in its wrappings.'

'What was in the coffin then?'

'An arm,' said Dame Lobelia. 'A withered, mummified arm severed just below the elbow.'

'How horrible!' said Katie. 'Poor arm.'

'Don't be daft,' said Josh. 'It was dead anyway.'

'I think the robbers must have been disturbed and had to make a sudden getaway. Anyway, the arm had been put back and the tomb closed up again in ancient times and from then on it lay undiscovered and forgotten, until I came along.'

There was a pause. Disappointment hung heavy in the air.

'So all the treasure had gone then?' said Josh.

'Not quite. When I un-wrapped the arm I found two matching amulets. Amulets of a kind that I had never seen before – and never have seen since, I might add. They were unique, in more ways than one.'

'Were they made of gold then, these amulets?' said Josh.

'No, no. It's not a question of what they were made *of* but of what they were made *for.*'

'What were they made for?'

'Can't you guess?' Dame Lobelia had a twinkle in her eye.

The children shook their heads.

'Why, to lift the curse of course! The curse written on the sarcophagus and coffin, the very curse that Katie copied. They and the inscription on them are your antidote young man.'

Chapter 10

'So that's the good news,' said Dame Lobelia. 'There is an antidote. It does exist. I have held it in my hands. And what is more I know it works because I've used it.'

'And the bad news?' said Josh.

'What makes you think there's bad news?'

'Because there usually is.'

'Now, there I can't agree with you,' said Dame Lobelia. 'Not as a general rule. But on this occasion, I must admit, you happen to be right. Anyway, now let me see… where did I get to in my story?'

'You'd just un-wrapped the arm,' said Katie, still fascinated by the ghoulish image.

'Ah yes, the arm...' She settled back in her chair once more and smoothed the folds of her skirt across her lap.

'Well, of course, I had no inkling of the true importance of the amulets at first. But I thought them rather curious so I put them to one side with the intention of studying them later. And then I must confess, in the confusion of what followed, I forgot all about them.

'We made tolerable progress for a day or two and then things started to go badly wrong. One morning, while we were working in the main chamber, part of the ceiling collapsed and seriously injured one of the workmen.

'Then, a couple of days later, I was aboveground sorting through some pottery finds while six of my best men were busy in the burial chamber, shoring up the ceiling to make it safe. Suddenly, from deep within the bowels of the tomb there came a cry that I can only describe as ...well... *inhuman*.' She paused as if recoiling from the memory.

'Moments later, the men came running out as if all the demons of the underworld were snapping at their heels!'

She gave a little shudder. 'The look on those men's faces! I hope I never live to see a look like that again. They came out gibbering wrecks. They had seen something down there and on no account could they be persuaded to go back in again. They quit work there and then, demanding that I immediately pay them what I owed them. And within an hour they were gone.'

'But what was it they saw?' said Andy.

'To this day I don't know,' said Dame Lobelia. 'And perhaps they hardly knew themselves, for they certainly never named it. But whatever it was, of one thing I am certain: it was evil, pure and simple. Unadulterated evil.'

The children tried to imagine unadulterated evil but it was difficult in that little suburban sitting room with the sunshine streaming in through the net curtains. Outside a blackbird in the hedge was calling sweetly to its mate.

'After that I was left with only three. I had to pay them double time of course. But it wasn't long before I lost another one... and in the strangest circumstances...' She paused to sip her cup of tea.

'You'd never think a man could die of *itching* would you?' She didn't seem to expect a reply for she immediately went on: 'Neither would I, had I not witnessed it myself. It started in his armpits...' (here there was a sharp intake of breath from Josh) 'and it spread, until his body was nothing but one red-raw, suppurating sore. The poor man couldn't rest or eat or sleep. And in the end he couldn't even think. By the time they came and took him to the hospital in Luxor he had completely lost his mind. I learned later that he fell into a coma and was dead within the week.'

Josh slumped a little in his chair. 'And what about the other two?'

'Oh, they refused to stay another night, of course. Double pay or not, they were determined to leave that very afternoon. I managed to prevail upon them, however, to help me crate up the last remaining objects from the tomb before they left.

'We hadn't got very far with our work, though, when the sky went strangely dark and a hot desert wind began to blow. Within minutes the air was filled with burning sand and we scrambled to our tents for shelter.

'When the storm was over I grabbed a shovel and struggled out, calling to my workmen. But silence was the only answer. I scoured the camp, shouting their names, but it seemed to be deserted.

'Then, up from the belly of the tomb, whose mouth was now half blocked with sand, there came a faint, unearthly sound. Had the workmen gone inside to shelter, I wondered, and were they now trapped behind a wall of sand?

'I struggled towards the entrance and began digging frantically with my shovel. Darkness was falling and the stars were beginning to rise.

'Suddenly, a fearful bellow echoed up from the depths below. It was that same inhuman cry that I had heard before, only louder now. Much louder.

'Terror froze me to the very core. I dropped my shovel and ran towards the jeep. But its wheels were sunk so deep into the sand that I knew I couldn't free them without help. In despair and panic I realised that I would have to stay — I would have to spend the night there on my own...' The old lady broke off abruptly. 'Would anybody care for some more tea?'

The children blinked as though suddenly awoken from a dream. They shook their heads.

'Surely someone would like this?' Dame Lobelia held up a plate on which languished a solitary chocolate biscuit. No one seemed to want it so she took it herself.

'Well,' she continued, 'I made myself as comfortable as I could that night (though I *did* go to bed fully dressed and with my boots on). I kept the lamp burning and, in case that should be extinguished, by my side I placed a powerful torch. Underneath my pillow was my pistol, fully loaded.

'Of course, there was no question of going to sleep, I was too afraid for that. Instead I did some very serious thinking about the suggestion of a curse. I already knew of its existence, since I had translated much of the hieroglyphic inscription on the sarcophagus and coffin, but I was still inclined to dismiss it all as superstitious nonsense. And I might have done so to this very day had it not been for what happened to me next.'

She paused and you could have heard a pin drop.

'It was about two in the morning and, despite my best endeavours to stay awake, I had drifted off to sleep. Suddenly, I became aware of scratching, scuffling sounds. At first I thought another sandstorm was in the offing. But then I realised that the sounds were coming from *inside* my tent.

'Unaccountably the lamp had extinguished itself and as I groped about in the darkness for my torch, to my unspeakable horror, my hand touched something cold and clammy…

'Such was my fragile state of mind that I'm afraid I screamed. And so loudly, that I even terrified myself! Eventually I found my torch and with trembling fingers switched it on whereupon instantly, like magic, everything went quiet.'

'Just like what happened to me!' cried Josh.

Dame Lobelia nodded. 'I did a thorough search but could find nothing. No scorpions or snakes, nothing.

'Well, as you may imagine this unnerved me quite a bit. So I decided to keep the torch switched on. Unbelievably, as though under the power of some soporific drug, I sank back into oblivion. But it was little less than an hour later that I awoke and this time I was fighting for my life! Somehow – and this is so extraordinary that I have never told another living soul of it 'til now – the lid of my locked and bolted trunk had been thrown open and the clothes that I had packed away inside had coiled themselves around my body like a snake. The breath was being squeezed out of my lungs and I was on the verge of suffocation. It was only with my last ounce of strength that I managed to wrench them off and hurl them to the farthest corner of my tent.

'When I was finally able to look about me I was amazed to see that everything was in a state of utter chaos. My clothes, my bedding, my papers – all the careful records of my excavations – had been scattered everywhere as if hurled about by some malevolent hand.

'It was then, at last, that it finally dawned on me that some supernatural power was at work. Something that no pistol could protect me from.

'Determined this time to stay awake and counting the hours left until the dawn I groped around on the floor for my papers. And then, in gathering them up, I found the amulets once more.

'This time I examined them properly. And then I realised something that had not occurred to me before. An extraordinary thing. They were not two amulets, but one.'

Andy frowned. 'How do you mean? How could two be one?'

'Well, each was half a circle you see. They were almost mirror images of each other. Almost, but not quite. Each half-circle bore an inscription, but the inscription was unfinished. Suddenly I saw the obvious. I saw that if I put the two halves together I would have not only a complete circle but also a complete inscription. I would, in fact, have the magic knot of *shen.*'

'What's that?' said Katie.

'Ah,' Dame Lobelia smiled as if talking of an old friend. 'The *shen* is a powerful symbol, a protector against evil. An eternal protector you see, because, being a circle, it has no end. Write your name and put it within the circle of the *shen* and you need fear nothing. But once the circle is broken, then the protection that it affords is scattered to the four winds. That was one of the reasons it was put there, of course, to give the curse more power – a thousand times more power! That's called reverse magic. It takes good and makes it into bad.'

'But what use is that to me?' demanded Josh. 'You said the amulets would lift the curse not make it worse!'

'Hold on!' said the old lady, raising her hands as if to ward him off. 'I haven't finished yet. What's broken can also be repaired, you know, with a little ingenuity. Reverse magic can itself be reversed, you see.'

Josh shook his head vigorously. 'No I don't see. I don't see at all.'

'Well, it's only common sense,' said Dame Lobelia. 'If a pot is broken you stick it together again with glue. If your clothes are torn you stitch them up with thread. If a thing is mended the good will replace the bad. Reversing reverse magic is much the same.

'It is simply a question of restoring the circle and making the inscription complete again. Good will then replace bad. A small ritual and incantation will act like glue or thread and – hey presto – the curse will be lifted!'

'Do you mean to say that that's all we have to do?' said Josh, leaning forward in excitement. 'Just put those amulets together and say some mumbo-jumbo and all this bad stuff will be over?'

'More or less,' said Dame Lobelia. 'That is what I did myself that night all those years ago. It came to me in a flash of insight – and it worked.'

'Well, could we go and get them now then and do it straight away?' asked Josh. 'I mean, if it's convenient – if you wouldn't mind. Only, if things keep going on like this much longer and stuff keeps getting broken I don't know what I'm going to do...' His voice trailed off. The look on Dame Lobelia's face was not encouraging. She got up and went over to a little bureau in the corner of the room. Lifting the lid she extracted from a drawer a small, battered cardboard box.

'This is all I have,' she said, opening it. The children peered inside and caught their breath. Nestling in a wad of cotton wool that had become yellow with age lay a curve of gleaming, dark stone, exquisitely wrought and engraved.

'It's beautiful,' breathed Katie, her eyes wide with admiration. 'But where's the other one?'

'Stolen,' said Dame Lobelia. 'That's the bad news.'

Chapter 11

'Stolen?' repeated Josh. 'But it can't be!'

'I'm afraid so,' sighed Dame Lobelia. 'Six months ago, from the British Museum. A gang posing as a party of visiting archaeologists got into the basement and made off with some very rare objects. They were obviously handpicked by someone in the know – an expert I'd say. A collector of unusual taste and discernment – like myself.'

'But what was it doing at the British Museum in the first place?' Josh was exasperated. 'I mean, why didn't *you* keep hold of it?'

'Too dangerous, don't you see? It's when they're near each other that they gather power. Kept apart they can't be used for anything – good *or* evil.

'It was the evil part that worried me,' she continued. 'After all, I'd seen what they could do when used for reverse magic hadn't I? I'd seen the power they could summon up to reinforce a curse – or any kind of spell or hex for that matter. I couldn't risk them falling into the wrong hands could I? So that was why I decided to keep quiet about the other one – the one I'd kept.'

'Well, that's that then!' Josh threw his arms up in despair. 'We're back where we started. Or rather, *I* am.'

'*Nil desperandum*,' said Dame Lobelia. 'Things could be a lot worse.'

'Oh really? How?'

'Well, to begin with, the amulet could be lost.'

'But it is,' he insisted. 'Or as good as – you just said it was stolen.'

'Stolen is not lost,' said Dame Lobelia. '*Lost* means in a ditch somewhere or down a drain or at the bottom of the sea or suchlike. But *stolen* – well that's another kettle of fish altogether.'

Josh stared at her, bewildered. She certainly had the oddest way of looking at things.

'When someone goes to all the trouble of stealing something as rare and valuable as this,' she went on, 'we can rest assured it's being taken care of. It'll be kept safe and sound until we can get our hands on it.'

'Get our hands on it?' said Josh. 'But we don't even know where it is.' He paused. He saw that she was smiling rather smugly. '...Or do we?'

'We might,' said the old lady, with a twinkle in her eye. 'There's a man I know of – rumours abound about him. Unsavoury rumours,' she added darkly. 'His name is Sir Sebastian Sedgewick. He's rich. Immensely rich. He could buy up all the houses in this street and it would mean as little to him as paying for a ticket on a bus would mean to us. He's ruthless too. I've heard he'll stop at nothing to get what he wants. And what he wants most of all are artefacts from ancient Egypt. The more unusual, the better. He'll go to any lengths, pay any price to get them. And it's said that what he can't get by paying for, he'll get by any other means he can.'

She paused to pour some milk from a little jug into her saucer. The cat, which had been sitting sphinx-like on

61

the windowsill, was beside her in a flash, tail up, brushing expectantly against her legs.

'There Bastet, that's for you, poor thing,' she said soothingly, laying the saucer down beside her feet. 'We've neglected you quite shamefully haven't we?' There came a loud, contented purr.

'Do you mean he *steals* them?' said Andy.

'Ten years ago it was the Barton-Poole Papyrus. He tried to buy it but the owner wouldn't sell. Next thing we heard, it had been stolen. Then there was the Berlin Funerary Vase. The owner wouldn't part with that and that too disappeared.'

'Could have been coincidence,' said Andy.

'Twice perhaps,' said Dame Lobelia. 'But three times? Most unlikely. Four years ago there was the distressing case of the Karnak Mummy Mask. That went missing, complete with mummy, from the Cairo Museum only two weeks after he had tried to buy it. They both disappeared into thin air and to this very day no one has seen hide nor hair of them.'

'So you think it's him then – this Sebastian Sedgewick – who took the amulet?' said Andy.

'I have no doubt of it. He's been after it for years. But the Trustees wouldn't sell. I think that he lost patience in the end and simply went and grabbed it.'

'But you've got no proof?'

'I don't need proof. I've got my intuition. I *know* it's him. It's just a case of getting inside that mansion of his and finding it.'

'He's got a mansion?' said Katie, wide-eyed with interest. 'Is it big?'

'Enormous I believe,' said Dame Lobelia. 'With battlements like a castle. And acres of parkland. And a wall around it at least three metres high. Barbed wire on the gates. And that's not to mention the guard dogs.'

'Walls, barbed wire, guard dogs... we'd never even get inside,' said Josh.

'*Nil desperandum,*' said Dame Lobelia. 'I have a plan...'

Katie started to interrupt. She had been wondering what *nil desperandum* meant... But Josh swiftly hushed her up. He was curious to hear just how an elderly lady was going to scale a three-metre wall and evade a pack of guard dogs.

'I had been feeling for some time that Sedgewick should be stopped,' she continued. 'But when the Karnak Mummy mask was stolen I knew I had to act. There was no telling what he might try next – Tutankhamun perhaps? I began to take steps to penetrate his defences. But Sedgewick isn't an easy man to get near. He keeps himself to himself. The only people who see him at all regularly are his closest staff – his butler and his housekeeper, a widow, Mrs Cherry.

'It was Mrs Cherry that I chose to target. I discovered that her favourite pastime on days off was playing bingo in the local town. I took to going there myself and we got to know each other quite well. In the end we got on famously. I called myself Mrs Cecilia Smith and I told her that I was staying with my sister in the area for a while. (Though I was in fact lodging at a B&B nearby.) I too was a widow, I said, fallen on hard times and should she hear of any vacancy in her line of work I should be glad to know about it.

'When I returned home we corresponded every now and then. For almost four months I had heard nothing from her, then last week I got this letter...'

She took a letter from the mantelpiece and began to read aloud:

'Dear Cecilia,

Just a short note to see how you are keeping and to say that I am feeling far from well myself. My rheumatism has been playing me up something chronic lately and I have had to tell Sir Sebastian that the job has got too much for me.

He was less than pleased, I can tell you, when he heard that I was going. Quite got on his high horse about it! "Mrs Cherry," he says, fixing me with that cold-fish stare of his, "this is really most inconvenient. How am I to find a replacement at such short notice?" He even threatened to stop all my back wages!

I said I was sorry but my joints couldn't stand another winter in that house. I told him I was off to Australia to stay with the daughter for a while. But I did add, you'll be pleased to hear, that I knew of just the woman who could take my place.

So the upshot, Cecilia, is this: should you want it, the job's as good as yours. I've said that you're a widow with no ties and he seemed extremely interested. He wants to see you for an interview. Two thirty on the twenty-fifth. Make sure that you're on time – he doesn't like to be kept waiting.

Warmest regards,
Dora.'

'The twenty-fifth?' said Andy. 'That's the day after tomorrow.'

'Perfect isn't it?' said Dame Lobelia. 'Interview on Monday. Move into Sedgewick Hall on Tuesday. Start

64

housekeeping on Wednesday – which will give me no end of opportunities for snooping – and by the weekend, well, I expect that we'll be home and dry and I'll have found the amulet.'

'If I survive that long,' said Josh.

'I have observed, young man, that optimism is not your strong point.' Dame Lobelia studied him intently. 'You really must cheer up, you know.'

'That's all right for you to say. You're not the one that's cursed.'

'You forget,' she said, 'that once I was.'

'Yes…well…' Josh looked suitably chastened. 'But at least you had the amulets. At least you could protect yourself.'

'And you will have protection too.'

She reached across to a shelf in the recess beside the fireplace and picked up a little alabaster casket covered in hieroglyphs. 'These should help to keep you safe.'

She offered him the box. He took it and then glanced at her, hesitating.

'Go on,' she said. 'Open it.'

The others leaned towards him, craning their necks to see. He lifted the lid and looked inside.

A human eye stared up at him. *The Eye of Ra!* He flinched. But no, he saw that it was only made of glass.

It lay on a bed of shining trinkets. Small pieces of finely polished stone cunningly carved into the shape of monstrous beasts. Rings minutely inscribed with hieroglyphs and set with the tiny heads of animals and birds.

'Ooh! That's lovely!' Katie reached in and took out a tiny golden fish, inlaid with a turquoise-coloured stone – the prettiest thing in the box.

'That's a charm against drowning,' said Dame Lobelia. 'It's very effective. He might do well to wear that in the bath.'

'*Him* wear it?' protested Katie, all thought of curses temporarily banished, 'It would look really nice on my bracelet that I got from…'

'And what's this?' Andy interrupted, holding up a little human-headed vulture. It had long hair, parted in the middle.

'A charm of general protection against the dark, chaotic forces of the underworld. That one he ought to keep beneath his pillow.'

'This one's over your front door,' said Josh.

'Ah yes, the *ankh*! That's an amulet of power – you should wear that at all times – never take it off. It will protect you when all the others fail.'

She picked out a little green crocodile and held it up against the window. The sun shone opaquely through it, lighting it up like a jewel. A fine silken cord was threaded through a small hole in its snout. 'This one is extremely good for warding off crocodiles. I've worn it many a time when travelling up the Nile.'

'Well, I'm not likely to be meeting many of those,' said Josh. Did she really think he was going to go around wearing all this junk?

'Crocodiles come in many different guises – remember the clippers?' A puzzled silence. She sighed at his slowness. 'What do you think of when you think of crocodiles?'

'Teeth,' said Katie.

'Teeth. Precisely!' said Dame Lobelia. 'Clippers have teeth don't they? Teeth of a sort, at any rate. Last time, you got off lightly – all you got was an ancient Egyptian priest's haircut. But next time you meet the crocodile you might not be so lucky.'

Josh said nothing. There was nothing you could say to a mad woman, he thought. Best just to act like you agreed with her and make your getaway as soon as possible.

'I think it would be wise to take it with you,' she went on, 'and one of these wouldn't go amiss either.' She held up a hideous little creature carved out of a piece of blood-red stone. Its grinning face – half ape, half man – had spiky teeth and great protruding eyes and from its scaly body sprang a pair of falcon's wings.

'If she thinks I'm wearing *that*,' he thought, 'she's got another thing coming!' But he took it meekly from her hands, without a word of protest.

In the end she selected for him three charms of power and three of general protection. All were threaded on a length of fine, strong cord and tied around his neck. He came away wearing them under his T-shirt and feeling very foolish even though no one else could see that they were there.

'I think that you'll have a more peaceful night tonight, Josh,' she said. 'Keep the charms with you at all times and you should be safe for the time being, provided that you're careful and don't take silly risks.'

She stood at the front door as they made their way down the path and out the gate. 'Goodbye!' she called. 'Watch for the post during the coming days. I'll write as soon as I've laid hands on...' she glanced about her, '...on you know what.' She waved to them and they waved back. And a moment later she had closed the door and was gone.

Chapter 12

Dame Lobelia was only half right. Josh *did* have a more peaceful night – once he actually got to bed – but the evening that went before it, turned out to be a stormy one.

Shoppers' Paradise had its usual effect on Dad's temper. And it didn't help that he had a blazing row about soft furnishings with Mum on the way home and almost crashed the car. Luckily, he didn't spot the damage to the sitting-room wall or the absence of the fruit bowl until the following day. And by then he was in a mellower mood anyway, because he was looking forward to a whole afternoon of golf.

But Josh's haircut was, unfortunately, impossible to miss. Dad was seriously disturbed by it. He went first white, then pink and then, when he began to shout, a vivid shade of puce. 'Skinhead!' and 'Juvenile delinquent!' and 'Like a blasted convict!' exploded in the air. Mum's reaction was much simpler. She merely took one look at Josh and screamed and dropped the plate of curry she was carrying.

Yet all in all, thought Josh, as he lay in bed on Sunday night, things could have turned out worse. There had been no 'happenings' for at least twenty-four hours now and he had the whole of the holidays to look forward to. He tucked the little vulture charm securely beneath his pillow and fingered the amulets that nestled comfortingly around his neck. Then, contentedly, he turned over, drifted off into a delicious sleep and dreamed about Melissa.

The next morning he slept late. When at last he woke he lay there for a while, eyes tight shut. Bright sunlight was flooding through the gap between the curtains. Gradually the sounds of the morning intruded in on him. He could hear Mrs Gribble clattering around in the kitchen below and chattering away, her voice mingling with Katie's piping tones. Suddenly alarm bells rang in Josh's head – Mum must have gone to work already! He leaned over and peered at the clock: ten-fifteen! They were meeting at Stanton Springs at half past ten!

There was no time for a shower – just a few generous squirts of *He-Man* and a quick brushing of the teeth. Then he threw on his jeans and T-shirt and was gone.

By the time he got to Stanton Springs the others were already mucking about in the pool. He watched them from the café terrace as he made his way towards the changing rooms, scanning the group for a glimpse of a certain person.

At last he spotted her. She was wading through the artificial waves around the pirate island and some boy – Michael Buss – was splashing her playfully. Laughingly she retaliated, sending up clouds of spray between them.

Josh stood and watched them. His free arm hung rigid by his side and his hand was clenched tightly in a fist. He felt a furious pounding in his chest. That Michael Buss – he'd show him! He was a better swimmer than him any day and he could dive better too. He'd show him!

He hurriedly changed and, as he stuffed his belongings into his locker, caught sight of himself in the full-length mirror opposite. Around his neck was a tangle of grotesque monstrosities. He looked ridiculous. How could he meet the others wearing those? Michael Buss would have a field day! He remembered how he'd taken the mickey out of Liam Donahue when he had come to school wearing one of his dad's gold chains around his neck. He stood there for a moment, hesitating, then he slipped the charms over his head and bundled them into his locker with the rest of his stuff.

By the time he got to the pool Melissa was doing a graceful crawl towards the deep end where the diving boards were. There was a group of girls from LV9 nearby, shrieking and giggling. Michael Buss and his sidekick, Adam Hooper, bobbed about like dolphins, splashing them and diving beneath the water to grab their legs and pull them under.

Suddenly they spotted Josh.

'Hey, look what's coming guys! It's baldy! Look at baldy!' shouted Michael Buss. There followed hoots of laughter.

'Nice haircut baldy!' yelled Adam Hooper.

'Yeah!' shrieked Francesca Hook, a tall, horse-faced girl, who had a crush on Michael Buss. 'Pity 'bout the face though!' There followed yet more peals of noisy mirth.

Melissa, who had reached the pool edge at the deep end, paused to have a look. Josh could feel the back of his neck go red, then his ears, then his face and then...he had this awful feeling that his head was changing colour too.

'Hi mate!' He felt a friendly arm descend around his shoulders. It was Eddie. 'You look really cool! I'm gonna get my mum to do me one like yours next time.'

Josh smiled back gratefully.

'Come on!' he grinned, 'Race you to the other end!' And he plunged into the pool, followed closely on his heels by Josh.

The two boys sliced through the water like a pair of small torpedoes. They were both strong swimmers but Josh usually had the edge. This morning, though, he felt as if he was ploughing through treacle. His body was a lead weight and a torpid languor suffused his limbs.

In the end Eddie beat him by a couple of heads. He reached the poolside panting furiously and feeling humiliated. Melissa and Kirsty were sitting on the edge a little further off, dangling their feet in the water. The two girls were watching him and every now and then they exchanged amused glances and spoke to each other in low tones.

Josh looked across at them and Melissa smiled at him. Once more he felt himself redden to the roots of his non-existent hair. Was she smiling at him or laughing at him he wondered? All of a sudden she slid into the water and swam past towards the shallow end. Without a moment's hesitation he followed her. She cut effortlessly through the water but he found it harder and harder to keep up.

Then he lost sight of her amongst the bobbing figures around the island. In front of him a group of little children were climbing on and off polystyrene floats. A small boy cut across him. His outstretched arms, swathed in a pair of water wings, were clinging on for dear life to an inflated plastic ring and he was kicking up a tremendous splash in his wake.

Josh stood up to get a better view around him. The water lapped his waist. He peered bewilderedly about. Where was Melissa? She seemed to have completely disappeared. He stood there, amongst the little kids, scanning the crowd and feeling vaguely foolish. Then, suddenly, something hit the back of his legs and his feet were swept violently from under him. He felt himself being dragged beneath the surface and, plunging under, caught a fleeting glimpse of a tangled mass of legs. He struggled up for air and something green and huge came bearing down upon him. Again he floundered, swallowing a mouthful of water as he sank. He seemed to stay down there for an eternity.

A great green shadow, like the belly of a ship, hovered over him and he couldn't find his way around it to the surface. Whichever way he moved it seemed to block him. He fought his way back up again and again it pushed him, coughing and spluttering, down, down to the depths and held him there...

The only thing he remembered – after they had pulled him up and before they'd dragged him onto dry land – was Melissa's frightened face...Melissa's frightened face and the gaping jaws and spiky teeth of a great green crocodile.

Chapter 13

'You all right son?' A tanned young man, dressed in trunks and a sweatshirt with the Stanton Springs logo emblazoned across the front, was bending over him. His face was full of concern. Josh managed to nod weakly between bouts of coughing. With help, he struggled up into a sitting position.

'What happened?' he said.

'You were trapped under that lilo there.' The lifeguard motioned with a sideways nod in the general direction of a small girl who was standing, weeping bitterly and being comforted by Kirsty and Melissa. Gripped tightly in her left hand was the tip of the tail of what appeared to be a slowly deflating, green crocodile.

'Those two girls got to you before me and managed to pull you out.'

Josh glanced towards them. Out of the corner of his eye he could see Buss and his cronies hovering a little further off, watching the proceedings.

He quickly looked away, groaning inwardly. Rescued! From the shallow end! *And by a couple of girls!* He'd never live it down! That lot would make his life a misery! Thank goodness it was the holidays and he wouldn't have to see them again for six weeks. There was just a chance that they might have forgotten about it by the time they had to go back to school. Fat chance, he thought, stealing a second glance in their direction. They were sniggering openly. No. They'd hold this one over him for months.

'Are you sure you're all right?' persisted the lifeguard. 'How's your breathing? Got any cramp? Would you like to go and see the nurse?'

'No, I'm fine, honestly,' insisted Josh, getting up a bit unsteadily. 'See – I'm okay.' Most of LV9 had got out of the pool to have a look and he was desperate to get away. If only the floor would conveniently open up and swallow him.

Help came in the lanky form of Eddie Pomroy.

'I'm bored of this pool,' he announced, loud enough for the others to hear. 'C'mon mate, let's go round to my house – I've got *Time Warp Traveller 2*.'

Little daggers of envy stabbed at the hearts of the onlookers. Everybody wanted *Time Warp Traveller 2*. It had only just come out.

The lifeguard, satisfied at last that Josh was unhurt, gave him a couple of parting pats on the shoulder. With Eddie beside him, and trying to look casual and unflustered, he made his way towards the changing rooms.

As he passed the girls he knew that he ought to stop and thank them, but he couldn't bring himself to do it – not in front of everyone. He kept on going, without so much as a glance in their direction.

By the time he reached his locker he wasn't feeling too proud of himself. But he didn't have to wait long to get his comeuppance.

No sooner had he turned the key in the door than, as though on a spring, it flew open and the entire contents hurled themselves towards his head. With a little cry he fell back, narrowly avoiding a flying trainer. The rest of his belongings hurtled past his left ear and landed in scattered heaps on the floor...

When he was over the first shock of it he glanced furtively about. But no one else had seen. Except for a couple of people in cubicles, the changing room was empty. Eddie was around the corner, busy at his locker.

Josh quickly scooped up his things and stood there, hugging them to his chest, feeling weak at the knees. He had realised something and it was a disturbing thought: *he wasn't safe anywhere.* First, he had almost drowned in the pool. And now things were flying at him like they did at home. What was going to happen next? Would he be run over by a bus outside the Leisure Centre or flattened by a piece of falling masonry as he passed the building site across the road?

And then another thought struck him. The charms! Where were they? He checked through the stuff that he was cradling in his arms but he couldn't find them. Panic seized him as he realised now that he was lost without them. What a fool he'd been not to wear them! He scanned the changing room but he couldn't see them on the floor. Where could they have gone? They couldn't just have disappeared into thin air.

He hunted on his hands and knees and suddenly saw something glinting in an empty cubicle by the showers. He went over and gave the door a cautious shove. It swung fully open and he was met by the faint odour of rotting flesh mingled with the smell of chlorine from the pool. He recognised it instantly and every fibre of his being told him to run.

But he couldn't move a muscle. Something was watching him. Something was glowing in the unnaturally deep shadow beneath the wooden bench that spanned the back of the cubicle. A red-hot coal. *An eye!* It seemed to sear into his brain, sucking out his energy and soldering him to the spot.

With an enormous effort of will he dragged his eyes from its burning gaze and focused on the charms. If only he could hook them out of the way and kick them back into the open space behind him! But he couldn't so much as lift his foot up off the floor.

Then something horrible happened. He sensed it more than saw it for he did not dare to let his eyes leave the charms. The thing *moved!*

It scuttled sideways. Once. Then again. Then a third time.

By a series of sudden, almost imperceptible, jerks it had moved right out from underneath the bench. All the while it fixed him with the eye as though to draw him by degrees into its fiery vortex.

Time stopped. All sound was blotted out. Nothing existed outside this metal box. Something hunched, toad-like and impenetrably dark was squatting in the middle of the cubicle…

A violent shove in the back sent him stumbling forwards. There was a moment of utter confusion. The sound of wildly scrabbling claws on tiles. Josh let out a yelp of terror. A cold, scaly weight scrambled across his bare feet and become entangled around his ankles. Then in a flash of movement it was gone and something fell clattering to the floor.

'Didn't mean to shove you *that* hard! You okay mate?' It was Eddie.

Josh panted, swallowing down his fear in little gulps.

'Yeah, just about!'

He steadied himself and then bent down to pick up the charms, quickly slipping them over his head.

'What the heck was that?'

'Dunno… Maybe a rat.'

Eddie looked alarmed. 'Are you sure?'

Josh shrugged his shoulders. Then, as relief flooded through him and the strength came pouring back, he managed a grin.

'Well, let's get out of here anyway,' said Eddie. 'I'm starving! What d'you say we go round my mum's shop first and get some money for a pizza?'

'Sounds good to me,' said Josh. And he headed for a cubicle to change, before his friend could comment on the strange collection of objects he was wearing around his neck.

***

On the way out Eddie stopped at one of the machines in the corridor to get a packet of crisps. Josh hung about waiting for him a little further off. Suddenly, he spotted Melissa. She was in the café buying something and she was on her own. His heart began to beat a little faster. Now was his chance to speak to her. He glanced at Eddie. He was fiddling with the buttons on the machine, trying to make it work. He could slip away, just for a moment, and Eddie wouldn't notice.

The blood was thumping in his chest as he made his way through the glass swing-doors of the café and strode purposefully towards her. His eyes were fixed on her and only her.

'Oi! RIDLEY!' It was Buss's voice, from a doorway at the other end. 'Wanna borrow my kid-sister's water wings next time do ya?'

Josh hesitated. His heart sank. Not again! Melissa turned around.

'But you'd better make sure you stay in the kiddies' pool just in case!' called Adam Hooper. ''Cause we don't want you drowning do we, baldy?' This caused much merriment amongst the cronies. Francesca Hook's snorting laughter could be heard clearly amongst the rest.

What was he to do now? Saying a soppy 'thank you' to Melissa in front of that lot would not be a good idea. But on the other hand, to turn around and go back out the door would be unthinkable.

He decided to ignore them and make out as if he'd just come in to buy a drink. He went up to the counter and stood beside Melissa.

'Hi,' he said.

She smiled warmly. 'Hi.'

'Good start,' he thought.

The large woman behind the counter moved towards him expectantly.

Michael Buss moved towards him too. 'Aren't we going to say thank you to the nice girlie for saving us, then?' He turned round to his cronies and they sniggered appreciatively.

Josh flushed a deep red and stared at the counter.

'What's the matter, baldy? Cat got your tongue?' called out Francesca Hook, with added venom, because she didn't like the way that Michael Buss was smiling at Melissa.

'No, it was a crocodile!' quipped Adam Hooper. And they all laughed.

'Perhaps he's still in shock,' said Buss. 'Does diddums want to see the nurse then?'

'Why don't you leave him alone!' Melissa turned on him angrily. 'You're *pathetic!*'

Buss was stunned into silence for a moment. He hadn't expected that. He had thought she rather liked him.

Francesca Hook, delighted and outraged at the same time, spat out: *'You're* the one that's pathetic, Melissa Butler! *You and Baldy!'*

Buss found his voice again. 'Yeah, *pathetic* – you're *pathetic,* Baldy! Hiding behind a *girlie!* Does he need a little girlie to protect him then?'

Josh turned to face him, fists clenched by his sides.

'Do you lot want to buy something or not?' The large woman behind the counter was frowning impatiently. 'Because if not, you can clear off. Especially you!' She glared pointedly at Buss.

'I'll have a cola please,' said Josh.

'Small or large?'

'Small.'

'That's right,' said Buss, smirking. *'Kiddie size.'*

'Look Buss, I'm warning you!'

'You hear that?' Buss turned to his sidekicks. 'He's *warning* us! Baldy's *warning* us. Oh, we're soooo scared!' There was another outbreak of sniggering.

'And what exactly are you warning us *about,* Baldy?' He smiled nastily.

'You'd just...' Josh swallowed hard. What was he doing? Buss was a good ten centimetres taller than him and almost twice as wide. '...You'd just better watch out, that's all!'

The other boy took a step towards him. 'Oh yeah? And who's gonna make me then?'

79

Francesca Hook giggled nervously.

'*I* am.' Josh tried not to look as scared as he felt.

Buss thrust his face so close that their noses almost touched. He spoke with quiet menace, slowly and deliberately. 'I'd like to see you try.'

They stood there, eyeball to eyeball, neither of them flinching. There's no turning back now, thought Josh with a sinking heart. I've got to fight him.

'RIGHT THAT'S IT!' The large woman was emerging from behind the counter, pushing up her sleeves. 'I've had enough of this! I'm having no fighting here!' She poked a chubby finger in Michael Buss's chest. '*You!* OUT!'

He backed off. She was considerably bigger than him, in all directions.

'But I want a drink too,' he said.

'Yeah, so do I,' said Adam Hooper.

'Yeah,' said Francesca Hook. 'We've as much right to be here as *them.*'

'And if you come back,' continued the woman, 'I'm calling Security and having you *thrown* out!'

They shuffled sulkily towards the swing doors and came face to face with Eddie coming the other way.

'*There* you are. I've been looking all over.' Eddie was half a head taller than anyone else in the class. Buss kept his distance.

'Well?' Eddie looked at Josh. 'You coming or what?'

Josh loitered for a moment. Then he turned to Melissa and smiled. 'See you then,' he said regretfully.

She drained her glass of cola and put it on the counter. 'Hold on,' she said, 'I'm coming too. I don't like the company round here.'

'We're busy,' said Eddie. 'We're going for a pizza.' Girls weren't part of his plans for the afternoon. How could you have a decent game of *Time Warp Traveller 2* with girls around?

'That's okay,' said Melissa. 'I like pizza – so does Kirsty.'

Eddie looked put out.

'Bye, bye Baldy. Don't fall in the paddling pool on your way out,' Michael Buss taunted softly as they passed.

But Josh didn't even hear. He was in seventh heaven. He and Melissa were going out to lunch.

Chapter 14

Mum and Dad had decided to get away from it all. Or, to be more precise, to get away from doing up the front room. Too many trips to *Shoppers' Paradise* had begun to take their toll and they couldn't agree on anything – not the colour of the paint, not the pattern on the wallpaper, not the carpet or the curtains or the furniture – not anything. When it got to the point that they were barely on speaking terms and divorce looked to be imminent Dad decided to take a stand.

He was home from work unusually late on Monday evening but when he walked through the front door his face was beaming. Tucked under his left arm was a brochure with a picture of the *Eiffel Tower* on the front. 'It'll be like a second honeymoon,' he said cheerfully. 'No kids and we can please ourselves for three glorious days.'

Mum looked dubious. 'Speaking of the children,' she said, 'what are we going to do with them?'

'It isn't fair!' complained Katie. 'Why can't we come?'

'Because it wouldn't be fair if you *did*,' snapped Dad. 'On *us*.'

'You wouldn't enjoy it anyway, Katie,' said Mum. 'Paris is just like London, full of cars and shops and people.'

'If it's just like London why are you going then?' said Katie.

'Because we need a break,' said Dad, 'from *you* lot.'

'Children need a break too,' persisted Katie, 'and we could go to Disneyland!'

'I'm not going to Paris for three days just to spend it all in an amusement park.'

'We needn't spend it *all* there,' said Katie. 'We could have two days there and one day shopping – for Mum.'

'Very generous of you,' said Dad. 'But you're not coming.'

Katie frowned sulkily. 'Well, what's going to happen to us then? You can't leave us on our own.'

'Yes they can – it'd be good!' exclaimed Josh. 'We could do as we like and eat pizza and chips every day.'

'You're not staying here,' said Dad. 'You're going to Deddbury.'

There was a chorus of groans from the boys. *'Not Auntie Alice!'*

'Your Aunt *has* kindly agreed to have you to stay for a few days, yes,' said their father. 'Which, considering the damage you did last time, is extremely good of her I might add.' He glared at Josh, 'Do you realise that dog was on tranquillising tablets for six months?'

'It was an accident!' protested Josh. 'I didn't mean to break the window. And it was just bad luck the ball landed in the dog basket.'

'*Poor* little Tickety-Boo,' said Katie, who had a soft spot for animals of every kind even Auntie Alice's Pekinese. 'He was having such a nice peaceful nap – you could hear him snoring all the way from upstairs. And then all of a sudden this great big football comes flying through the window and falls, plonk, on top of him. He didn't stop shaking for half an hour did he Andy? And when Auntie Alice tried to pick him up he bit her, do you remember?'

'Yeah,' grinned Andy.

'Well, there'll be no football this time,' said Dad, 'or loud music either. It upsets the dogs.'

'That does it then!' Josh folded his arms defiantly. '*I*'m not going!'

'Me neither!' said Andy.

'I've said you're going and you're going,' said Dad.

'But there's nothing to do there,' said Andy. 'There's no TV and she makes us go to bed at half-past eight like Katie.'

'Too bad, it's all arranged. I've already booked the seats on Eurostar.'

'Well, that's too bad for you then, isn't it?' said Josh. ''Cause *we're* not going.'

Mr Ridley glared at his sons. He cast about in his mind for something suitably stern and disciplinarian to say.

'Well, I *like* going to Auntie's,' said Katie. 'We go on country rambles looking for wild flowers and we do jigsaw puzzles after supper and she lets us take the dear little dogs for walks and ...'

'*Dear little dogs!*' Josh almost spat out the words. 'Dribbling, drooling, pop-eyed things! The two put together wouldn't make one decent-sized dog. I'd rather take a rat out on a lead.'

'As a matter of interest,' Mum said suddenly, 'how come she agreed to have them?'

Her husband looked uncomfortable.

'Well?'

'It's only for a week.'

'What's only for a week?' Mum's worst suspicions were immediately aroused. 'What did you promise in return?'

Her husband's eyes darted nervously about the room, unwilling to meet her gaze.

'What did you promise in return?' she repeated, rather louder than the first time.

'Now, don't go getting upset…'

'William!' barked Mum. *'Answer me!'*

Dad sighed. He had hoped to leave it until she was in a better mood, but now there was no help for it. He would have to spill the beans. 'We're having the Pekinese next month while she's away in Spain.'

There were gasps of horror all round. But Katie's face lit up with delight.

Mum was now, indeed, upset. 'William, how *could* you! You *know* what happened last time!'

'Yes, yes,' he said quickly, 'I've been thinking about that and I've come up with a solution. If I put one of those wire baskets over the letterbox on the inside of the door — that'll protect the postman's hand and the letters too.'

But Mum had other objections. 'And the curtains?' she demanded. 'What will protect *those*? Three times that animal lifted its leg against those curtains in the front room. *Three times!* That's why we're getting new ones in case you'd forgotten?'

'Oh, she'll pay for any dry-cleaning, naturally,' said Dad. 'But it won't come to that,' he added. 'The kids will keep an eye on the beasts and make sure they don't go anywhere near the curtains…'

'Huh!' Josh snorted derisively at the very idea. But Katie nodded enthusiastically. She would thoroughly enjoy looking after the dear little dogs when they arrived.

'I don't know…' Mum was unconvinced. 'I still don't like it…'

'Don't worry, Mum,' said Josh, 'they won't be coming anyway. 'Cause us lot won't be going.'

But something happened the next morning to make him change his mind.

***

The envelope was addressed to Josh, but there was something about the elegantly sloping handwriting that made Andy pick it up off the doormat and pocket it quickly before anyone else had a chance to see.

Once both parents were safely out of the house he called Josh and Katie into the privacy of his bedroom. He hung up his 'KEEP OUT' and 'DO NOT DISTURB' signs on the outside of his door in the hope that they would ward off Mrs Gribble and her vacuum cleaner for a while. Then he handed his brother the letter.

Josh hesitated. It had been a full three weeks since the 'happenings' and the meeting with Dame Lobelia. Were it not for the charms that he took care never to leave off wearing, he could almost believe that it had all been nothing but a bad dream.

'Go on!' urged Andy. 'Open it!'

He slid his finger under the corner of the flap and tore it open. The cream-coloured paper felt thick and expensive. Across the top was some sort of crest depicting an eagle, or perhaps a vulture, with wings outstretched. And beneath that, in gold embossed lettering, was the address: *Sedgewick Hall, Coomley Heath, Northamptonshire*. Dame Lobelia had got the job.

'Well?' said Katie. 'Is it her?'

Her brother nodded.

'Well, go on. Read it then.'

The distant roar of the vacuum cleaner could be heard from downstairs. In a low voice Josh began:

'My dear young friends,

Here, at last, is the letter I promised you. As you see I am now established as housekeeper at Sedgewick Hall – although it has taken me longer than I expected to settle in and get my bearings.

This house is truly enormous! Indeed it may, I suspect, be even bigger than it looks. For although I seem to have been over every inch of the place there are, I am convinced, parts of it that I have yet to see. From time to time I have heard things that I can't explain – footsteps in empty rooms, mutterings from the walls. Unless the place is haunted (which of course I don't rule out) I can only guess that it must be honeycombed with secret passageways. At any rate, one thing is certain: this house is full of surprises.

And so is Sir Sebastian. He is forever turning up where I least expect to see him. My second morning here was a case in point. I had just left him in his study, having received my instructions for the day, when on passing by the library door I thought I'd go inside and change some flowers. Imagine my amazement, therefore when, upon entering, I found that he had got there before me! There is only one entrance to the library (as far as I know) and to reach it he would have had to pass me in the hall. But –

and this is the extraordinary part – I am certain he did not!

As for the amulet – I am convinced that it is here. I have its twin with me and it seems to sense the nearness of the other. Last night it glowed with a pale violet light as I held it in my hand and it felt warm as though it was gathering power again. But exactly where the other is, I can't yet say. Maybe it's in some part of the house that I have overlooked or perhaps in some secret place that I have yet to discover. It certainly is a puzzle and I think I'll need your help to solve it.

I must sign off now, if I'm to catch the post in Coomley. It's too risky to telephone you from the Hall so I will use the phone box in the village when I go in to collect the groceries on Tuesday morning. Expect my call at ten o'clock. Should someone other than one of you pick up the receiver I will say it is a wrong number and try again the following day. But do try to make sure that you are ready when I ring. Time is of the essence, my young friends; the power of the charms is not inexhaustible. We must delay no longer than is absolutely necessary.

Yours, with all good wishes,
Lobelia Carter-Smythe.

P.S. Nil desperandum!'

'What does she mean: "the power of the charms is not inexaustible"?' said Josh, anxiously fingering the trinkets around his neck. 'Do you think they might stop working?'

But the others didn't answer. They were listening to something else. Downstairs the vacuum cleaner had been switched off and the shrill bell of a telephone could be

heard. Andy looked down at his wrist. His watch said ten
o'clock.

Chapter 15

Mrs Gribble, duster in hand, was already in the hall and plodding purposefully towards the telephone when Andy reached the top of the stairs. He almost flew down, his feet barely brushing the treads as he went. Then he sped past her and grabbed the phone just before she got to it.

'Good grief! You're in a hurry!'

Andy hugged the receiver to his chest. 'It's all right. It's for me,' he said.

'Well, it must be someone special,' laughed Mrs Gribble. 'I've never seen anyone move so fast!' She shook her head in mock amazement and turned back towards the sitting room.

He waited until she had closed the door behind her before he said 'Hello.'

There was a pause at the other end. 'Hello? Who's that I'm speaking to?' It sounded like Dame Lobelia.

Another pause.

'Is that you Andy?' It was definitely Dame Lobelia's voice.

'Yes, it's me.'

'Oh, thank goodness! Now listen – I can't talk for long in case I'm seen – but I think I'm onto something with regard to you know what...'

'You've found it!'

'No, but I think I may be close. Very close. But I'm going to need your help. Sir Sebastian is off on a business trip this weekend and I'm trying to think of some way to get you all up here.'

'Not a chance,' said Andy. 'Mum and Dad are going to Paris this weekend and we've got to go and stay with our aunt.'

'Your *aunt?*' She sounded dismayed. 'Where?'

'A place called Little Deddbury.'

'*Little Deddbury?*' Dame Lobelia sounded intrigued.

'It's a village in the country,' said Andy. 'Not far from Amersham.'

'I know,' said Dame Lobelia.

'Oh I forgot,' said Andy, 'you used to live there didn't you?'

'I did indeed. A charming little place.'

'Well, Josh doesn't think so and neither do I. We hate it. We've said we're not going. We can't stand her! She's banned football and there's no TV and we have to go to bed at a ridiculous time. But I expect Dad'll *make* us go in the end because they've already got the tickets and we're having the Pekinese...'

'I'm sorry, you've entirely lost me,' interrupted Dame Lobelia. 'What have Pekinese to do with anything?'

'That's the deal,' said Andy. 'We're having Auntie Alice's Pekinese while she goes away, if she has us while Mum and Dad go away.'

'Did you say *Alice?*' she said sharply.

'Yes.'

'Hmmm...and is she an *un*married lady, this Auntie Alice of yours?'

'Well...yes,' said Andy, 'she is.'

'On your *father's* side of the family?'

'Yes.'

'Member of the Women's Institute?' She was warming to her theme. 'Keen on dogs?'

'Well, I've said she's got Pekinese,' said Andy, 'but I don't know about the other thing.'

'Not keen on children though?'

'No. Not on us, anyway. Look, what's all this about...?'

'Excellent!' said Dame Lobelia. 'Could hardly be better! What a stroke of luck!'

'I don't get it. *What's* a stroke of luck?'

'I know her!' said Dame Lobelia. 'Alice Ridley. We used to belong to the same branch of the WI.'

'*Dreadful* woman,' she added cheerfully.

Andy was confused. How it could be such a cause for celebration that she knew Auntie Alice if she thought that she was dreadful? 'I don't understand. Why do you say...?'

'Oh!' There was a sudden note of alarm in Dame Lobelia's voice. 'There's someone coming – Mortlock from the Hall!'

Her tone became low and urgent. 'Now listen, quickly,' she said. 'Tell your brother that he's got to go to Deddbury – that his future depends upon it.'

'But why?' said Andy.

'I can't explain now.'

'Why don't you tell him yourself – he's just here...'

'There isn't time.'

'But he won't take it from *me*.' said Andy.

'Of course he will,' insisted Dame Lobelia. 'He knows you're not a fool – otherwise we would never have met. Just you all go off to Alice's like dutiful children and wait until you hear from me. Oh…and I almost forgot,' she added. 'Take the football along…and USE it!'

'But…'

'Goodbye…' And she hung up.

***

No one was more surprised than Dad when the boys suddenly changed their minds. He had tried all manner of threats, bribery and corruption to get them to agree to go to Little Deddbury, but nothing seemed to work. He was just beginning to think that he might be forced to cancel the trip and go back to arguing about wallpaper with his wife when they suddenly gave in.

'I knew you'd see sense in the end,' he said cheerfully, as he steered the car around the final bend in Fenders Lane before *Mon Repos* cottage came into view. He pulled up outside his sister's green front door and got out, breathing deeply.

'Mmmm…smell that country air,' he said as a tractor and trailer loaded with farmyard manure trundled past. 'And you didn't want to come!' He looked at the boys pityingly.

'Listen!' He cocked his head in the direction of a nearby field where sheep were bleating. 'Listen to those country sounds! You won't hear *those* in London!'

A sudden explosion of barking erupted behind the green front door. Auntie Alice's Pekinese had become aware that someone was actually daring to loiter in the road outside their house. A moment later the door opened and Auntie Alice poked her head around it. Instantly, two mop-like objects on legs, charged out from under her. They made straight for Mr Ridley's shins.

***

'You can't blame *them,*' said Alice, when at last they had managed to disentangle the dogs from her brother's tattered turn-ups and were recovering with a cup of tea. 'They thought you were the postman. What did you want to go hanging about out there like *he* does for?'

'I'm not surprised he hangs about,' said Dad as he drained his second cup. He still felt rather shaken. 'I expect it takes the poor devil quite a while to screw up the courage to put your letters through.'

'They're only following their instincts. They're guarding their territory. But I wouldn't expect you to understand,' said his sister, 'not having animals of your own.'

'We did have a goldfish,' said Katie.

'Did you dear?'

'Yes. He died though.'

'Oh, I'm sorry to hear that dear,' said Auntie Alice, trying to sound sincere. 'How very sad.'

'Yes, it was. But we did give him a funeral.'

'Really?' said Auntie Alice, suppressing a yawn and thinking how boring children were compared with dogs. 'And did you bury him in the garden?'

'No,' said Katie. 'I mummified him.'

Auntie Alice blanched. 'You…you …did…*what?*'

'Well, I think I'd better be off now,' said Dad, getting up rather suddenly. 'Last minute packing to do, you know. Train to catch this evening.'

'Did she just say…?' His sister seemed to be in shock.

'Don't bother to show me out, I know the way.' And he was off out the door before they even had a chance to say goodbye.

Auntie Alice remained in shock for the whole of that afternoon and most of the following morning. It wasn't exclusively Katie's fault. The others played their part.

Her opinion of the oldest one – as a great clumsy oaf – was soon confirmed. Within hours of being in her lovely home he had succeeded in wrecking something that she had been working on for weeks. Her giant jigsaw puzzle of the Taj Mahal.

Ching-Ching had just spotted a cat in the garden at the time. He was quite properly making a beeline for the patio doors in order to see it off, when that wretched boy got in his way and tripped. The stupid fool had grabbed onto the table to break his fall and had managed to tip her jigsaw all over the floor. Just when she had all but completed it too! She almost cried when she saw it lying there, scattered all over the carpet, with Ching-Ching, sitting in the middle of it all, chewing the top off one of the minarets.

Then, after tea, the middle one had suddenly produced a football and started kicking it around the garden. Poor little Tickety-Boo had run cowering and quaking behind the sofa. And she had finally lost her temper. She had torn outside in a towering rage, scooped up the ball and flung it into the dustbin.

On top of this there had been other misdemeanours. Someone – she suspected Katie – had left a bar of chocolate melting in the sun on the sofa in the lounge and then had gone and sat on it. There were sticky finger marks on the furniture and sweet papers beneath the chairs. A tap had been left dripping into the soap dish in the bathroom dissolving the bar into a gluey mush. And two smelly socks had somehow found their way onto the landing by the stairs. But all of this was as nothing compared with what occurred with Next Door's dog the following morning.

Next door there was a 'lady dog' (as Auntie Alice insisted on describing it) that Tickety-Boo was keen to get to know. Auntie Alice and Next Door, on the other hand, were equally keen that the two should have not even so much as a passing acquaintance.

'I don't see why they can't play together and be friends,' Katie had said. 'It would be lovely. We could take them all out for walks.'

Auntie Alice had replied that, on the contrary, it would not be lovely and that there might be deeply deplorable consequences. Only she wouldn't say what.

Tickety-Boo, however, was in love and he was determined to get at the object of his passion. He tried digging a hole under the fence, which was duly blocked up with stones from the rockery. He tried squeezing through a narrow gap between the wooden uprights. And then got stuck half way. He tried making a run for it when Auntie Alice opened the front door to take the milk in. But Next Door's gate was shut. And in between it all he whined pitifully.

Then, finally, he managed it. And it was all those wretched children's fault Auntie Alice reflected bitterly when, later, she was presented with the consequences. If the little one hadn't kept pestering her to be allowed to take them out for walkies and the older ones hadn't been in the way so much of the time it might never have happened at all. As it was, what with the children's misbehaviour and Tickety-Boo's constant whining, she was only too glad to get rid of them all.

They set off down the lane, Katie with Ching-Ching and Andy with Tickety-Boo. Josh having refused to have anything to do with either of them.

'I can't stand much more of this,' he moaned, once they were out of sight of *Mon Repos*. 'That woman's an evil old bag! It's like being in a torture camp and I'm bored out of my mind. And as for these so-called dogs…' he aimed a mock kick at Tickety-Boo's waddling behind. Just at that moment, however, having rounded a sharp bend in the tree-lined lane, they came face to face with Next Door's dog.

Tickety-Boo launched himself joyfully at his heart's desire and pandemonium ensued. Next Door's dog, it appeared, wanted nothing whatever to do with him. The air was rent by a terrifying explosion of snarling and squealing and gnashing of teeth. Next Door dropped the lead in panic and booted the interloper in the rear. But Tickety-Boo seemed impervious to pain.

It was then that Next Door's dog decided to make a run for it. She dashed blindly across the road and into a coppice bisected by a little brook. It was all over before anybody had a chance to realise what was happening. Tickety-Boo gave a mighty tug on his lead, yanked it out of Andy's grip and set off in hot pursuit.

***

'You stupid, stupid boy!' cried Auntie Alice. 'How *could* you let him go!'

Tickety-Boo had been missing for almost an hour. And they had all been trudging through ditches and fields and woodland looking for him and calling out his name.

'It wasn't my fault,' protested Andy. 'He took me by surprise. He's as strong as an ox.'

'I'm sure he'll turn up,' said Josh. 'Like the other one did. You wait 'til he gets hungry.'

Next Door's dog, muddy and dishevelled, but otherwise apparently unharmed, had indeed turned up half an hour earlier. But there was still no sign of Tickety-Boo so they had set off to look for him.

Auntie Alice was quivering with indignation. 'We're going home right now,' she said. 'I'm going to phone your parents in Paris and tell them to come back immediately and take you all away. You're quite beyond the control of any normal human being!'

She turned back towards the cottage and the children plodded miserably after her. The thought had occurred to all of them that there might be something even worse than staying at Auntie Alice's. And that was having your parents cut their holiday short to come and take you home. They couldn't even begin to imagine what Dad would have to say when he came and got them. It didn't bear thinking about.

They followed her into the sitting room and sat watching glumly as she rifled through some papers near the telephone. Then, having found the number she was looking for, she lifted the receiver and began to press the buttons...

'Trrrrring!' The imperious ring of the doorbell sent Ching-Ching rushing, barking into the hall. Auntie Alice, sighing in exasperation, replaced the receiver and went to answer it. The children stayed put and exchanged anguished glances. A moment later, hearing cries of joy and even wilder barking, they too ventured into the hall to see what all the fuss was about.

A matted and bedraggled Tickety-Boo was wriggling happily in Auntie Alice's arms. He wagged his tail and licked her face, while she told him how glad she was to have him back. The lady who had brought him home stood smiling in the doorway. She gave the children a conspiratorial wink. It was Dame Lobelia Carter-Smythe.

Chapter 16

'What a blessing that you happened to come along when you did,' said Auntie Alice. 'Five minutes earlier or later and you might have missed the precious darling and then where would we be?'

She sat with the 'precious darling' on her lap feeding him *Doggichockies,* which he wolfed down greedily. Each time she took another from the bag he licked his chops expectantly, sprinkling little drops of saliva onto her skirt.

'Yes,' said Dame Lobelia. 'I had just turned the corner and there he was, coming out of a thicket by the side of the road. I recognised him immediately.'

'Of course you did. Anyone would,' said Auntie Alice. 'He's not your ordinary run-of-the-mill sort of dog.' She hugged him. 'You're a very special little doggie, aren't you Tickety-Boo?' She drew out another *Doggichockie* from the bag and held it up. His watery eyes looked from it to her in mute appeal.

'It almost seemed like fate,' reflected Dame Lobelia. 'And then, to come here and find that you have staying with you none other than my own charming, young friends. It's really quite an extraordinary coincidence.'

'Well, there I *can't* agree with you.' She gave her visitor a hostile stare and Dame Lobelia was immediately disconcerted. Could it possibly be that Alice suspected something?

'Er...how do you mean?' she said, glancing out of the window at where the children sat talking in a huddle on the patio steps.

'Well, personally, I find them far from "charming". They've been nothing but trouble since they got here.'

'Oh surely not,' said Dame Lobelia, much relieved that that was all she meant.

'I'm afraid so,' and she proceeded to list their numerous offences.

'In fact, I was on the verge of phoning their parents to come and take them home when you arrived.' She put a hand up to her forehead. 'I'm at my wits' end. My nerves won't stand much more.'

'I can see your point of view I must admit,' said Dame Lobelia. 'Bringing that football here again, after what happened last time, does show a certain lack of feeling.'

Auntie Alice pursed her lips and nodded. 'And I'm not sure now that I'd feel safe leaving my darlings with those horrors when I go to Spain anyway, to be honest with you Lobelia. Especially after this morning. I mean anything might have happened! Poor little Tickety-Boo could have been run over! If it wasn't for the fact that the holiday's all paid for and I'd never get my money back I'd cancel it today ...'

Dame Lobelia hastily interrupted her: 'Oh, but what happened today was due to unusual circumstances, Alice, what with the dog next door and everything. Don't forget that your brother and his wife will be in charge, not the children. The little dogs will be perfectly safe I'm sure.'

'Well, I suppose so, yes,' said Alice, somewhat mollified. 'But the fact remains that my nerves are shot to pieces already and these savages have been here for barely twenty-four hours. I simply have no alternative but to call their parents and tell them to come and take them home straight away.'

'Well I wouldn't act too hastily if I were you,' said Dame Lobelia. 'After all you need your holiday more than ever now, don't you? Besides, I can't see your brother agreeing to have the dogs for a week if you go cutting short his trip to Paris, you know.'

'But surely he wouldn't be so unreasonable as to go back on our arrangement?'

'Well, I can see your point of view of course,' said Dame Lobelia. 'But *he* might not you know. *He* might see it differently. *He* might feel that you'd broken your side of the bargain, so to speak.'

'But that's ridiculous!' Alice exclaimed. 'How can I be the one to blame? He promised me his children would behave!'

Dame Lobelia shrugged her shoulders sympathetically and sighed.

'But what am I to do then?' said Alice.

'Are there no alternatives for the dear little dogs?'

'*Kennels* do you mean?' Alice was outraged. 'I would never consider them! Never! They're far too highly strung!'

'Oh dear. And is there no one else?' asked Dame Lobelia. 'What about that – what's her name – that woman up the road?'

'Stella Cribbage? No! Never in a thousand years! Not after all that fuss she made about her sofa last time! Poor Tickety-Boo was simply marking out his territory.'

'But her sofa wasn't his territory,' said Dame Lobelia.

'It was for the time being – that's dog psychology,' said Alice.

'Yes, I see,' mused Dame Lobelia. 'But where does all this leave us now?'

'With no alternative but to send them to my brother's while I'm away in Spain.'

'In that case, then, couldn't you find it in yourself to put up with the children for just a little longer? It's only for a few days.'

'No! Absolutely not! The girl is just about tolerable. But those boys are oafs. Even one more day of them would make me ill.'

There seemed to be no way out of the dilemma and the conversation dwindled into silence. Dame Lobelia got up and paced about the room, making a great show of appearing to be thinking very hard. She put her hands together, as if in prayer and rested her chin on her fingertips.

At length she gave a little cry of triumph. 'I've got it!' she exclaimed, so suddenly that Alice started violently and Tickety-Boo fell off her lap. 'Why don't I have them instead?'

'Oh, Lobelia *would* you? Would you really?' Alice's face flushed pink with gratitude. 'They're no trouble at all to feed – just a tin of *Happychappy Chunks* a day and some *Small Bite Mix*, that's all they need.'

'I meant the *children*,' said Dame Lobelia.

'The *children*?' She looked astonished. 'Not the *dogs*? Are you *sure*?'

Dame Lobelia nodded. 'The children and I get along famously, so it's no trouble to me. It's the perfect solution. Their parents can continue with their holiday, you can rest your nerves and the dogs can still go and stay with your brother while you're away in Spain.'

'Get along famously...' repeated Alice, as if this was the most extraordinary thing she had ever heard in her life. 'Lobelia, are you *sure* you wouldn't prefer the dogs?'

The other smiled and shook her head. 'You forget I have a cat.'

'But what will you *do* with them Lobelia?' persisted Alice. 'In that tiny house of yours with all those bits and pieces you've got lying around. They'll break the lot Lobelia – you should have seen my jigsaw. No, I really cannot let you do it Lobelia it simply wouldn't be fair.'

'Don't worry about my artefacts,' said Dame Lobelia, increasingly alarmed that her plan might go awry. 'We won't be going home we'll take a little trip – to the coast somewhere – I need a break myself – it will be thoroughly delightful.'

Alice looked at her aghast. 'A little trip?' With *those* three? And she thought it would be 'thoroughly delightful'? The woman must be mad! 'However,' she reflected, 'it was tempting...it really would be most convenient.'

'Well...I suppose... if you really don't mind.' Alice went over to the telephone and lifted the receiver.

'What are you doing?'

'Phoning their parents, of course, to tell them.'

'I wouldn't do that if were you,' said Dame Lobelia, hastily pressing the cut-off button.

'Why ever not? I can't just hand them over without a word to anyone.'

'My dear Alice, think for a moment. If you do tell them, what will they say when it's time for them to look after the dear little dogs next month?'

Alice looked blank.

'They'll refuse to do it, won't they?' said Dame Lobelia.

'I don't see why,' said Alice. 'The children will still have been looked after…'

'But not by *you*. And that's the point. They'll have the perfect excuse to go back on their promise. Or even worse, to send the dear little dogs to kennels while you're away.'

At the mention of the word 'kennels' Alice's face assumed first a stricken expression and then one of grim determination and she said: 'You're absolutely right Lobelia! We *won't* tell them. That brother of mine will jump at any excuse to wriggle out of his obligations – and his wife is even worse. Just you make sure that you get them back here in time for when he comes to pick them up on Sunday evening. And no one but us and the children need be any the wiser.'

'Exactly,' said Dame Lobelia. 'Alice, my dear, I couldn't have put it better myself. It's foolproof.'

Chapter 17

In less than half an hour they were packed and on their way, crammed into Dame Lobelia's battered, old Morris Minor. When they had rounded the bend in Fenders Lane and *Mon Repos* had disappeared from sight the children punched the air and whooped with joy.

'How did you manage it?'

'What did you *say* to her?'

'Are we *really* going to Sedgewick Hall?'

'One at a time with all your questions! One at a time!' laughed Dame Lobelia.

They took the scenic route and kept to minor roads, where woods and hedge-rimmed fields meandered by. The sun was shining brightly and a sparkling morning had mellowed into a golden afternoon. At length, they wound their way down a shady lane under a canopy of overarching trees and turned into a sleepy little village with a duck pond in the middle of its green.

'I think we'll stop here and have some lunch,' said Dame Lobelia, pulling up beside a quaint old inn with whitewashed walls and roses around its door.

'Auntie Alice has kindly provided us with some meat-paste sandwiches, I believe.' She reached down behind her seat and picked up a plastic carrier bag in which were several foil-wrapped packs.

Josh opened one and pulled apart a sandwich. He made a face. 'Looks like *Happychappy Chunks,*' he said. He wrinkled his nose. 'Smells like it too.'

'I'm not hungry,' said Andy.

'Me neither,' said Josh.

'I feel sick,' said Katie.

'Oh, *what* a pity,' said Dame Lobelia, a mischievous twinkle in her eye. 'And I was so looking forward to having a slap-up lunch in this delightful inn here. And to feeding these,' she held up a sandwich that was curling at its edges, 'to the ducks.'

***

They did have a slap-up lunch: a delicious roast with gravy and new season's vegetables and potatoes that were fluffy on the inside and crisp and crunchy on the outside. Afterwards, there was an array of apple pies and strawberry tarts and summer puddings and ice-cream sundaes for them to choose from so that, by the end, they were completely stuffed and couldn't move. Dame Lobelia drank half a pot of coffee and then suggested a walk. They wandered in the inn's delightful garden and found some recliners beside the stream that ran along its southern border. Dame Lobelia treated herself to a cigar, leaned back in her chair and puffed contentedly. The aromatic smoke curled out across the water.

'You shouldn't smoke, it's very bad for you,' said Katie, suddenly roused out of her after-dinner torpor. 'When I went to the Natural History Museum…'

'Oh, don't start *that* again,' groaned Josh. He was beginning to feel a little queasy. He was afraid that he might have overdone it with that second helping of pudding.

'You're absolutely right,' said Dame Lobelia, not at all offended by the rebuke. 'It's a filthy habit. But I do it very rarely and only when I need to think. And at the moment, my dear Katie, I'm having to do quite a bit of thinking.'

'About "you know what" do you mean?' said Andy, first taking a precautionary look around him, to make sure that they weren't being overheard.

'Precisely,' said Dame Lobelia. 'And I think it's time we discussed our plans, don't you?'

They nodded eagerly.

'Now, as I told you in the car, as far as they're concerned at Sedgewick Hall you three are all my grandchildren, come to visit me while Sir Sebastian's away.'

'He does know about us, though?' said Andy.

'Oh yes, he knows all right. Although he's none too pleased you're coming. He isn't fond of children (like someone else we know). He was afraid that you might break something so I had to promise you'd be on your best behaviour.' She chuckled. 'Though I didn't give him any assurances about my *own*.'

'Now, one thing is vital,' she continued, lowering her voice. 'It's something you must not forget – whenever anyone's about you must refer to me as "Grandma" and *never* as "Dame Lobelia". There could be serious consequences if you let slip my real name. Do you understand?'

They nodded.

'If anyone suspects that we are not who we appear to be we'll be instantly thrown out. Or worse. And then our chances of getting our hands on "you know what" will be absolutely nil. Do I make myself quite clear?'

They nodded again.

'What do you mean "or worse"?' enquired Katie.

Dame Lobelia looked sombre. 'I'm not sure what I mean,' she said, 'except to say that Sir Sebastian is a very dangerous man. A man not to be trifled with. And we must take care to watch our step at every turn and not make silly mistakes.'

There was silence for a moment while they considered this. Then Andy said: 'What did you mean on the phone about being on to something?'

'Ah, *that!*' Her eyes lit up. This 'something' seemed to be of great importance. She paused to take another puff of her cigar. 'Do you recall the incident concerning the library that I mentioned in my letter?'

'Yes.'

'Well, something similar occurred last week. I happened to see him go in there again, only he didn't know I'd seen him. And this time I decided to keep watch. I loitered in the hall, pretending to be polishing up the brassware by the fireplace. All the while, though, I was keeping my eyes firmly fixed on that library door. He had been inside for half an hour or so when, suddenly, as large as life and twice as ugly, he emerged, not from the library, but from the door across the hall. And what was more, he was carrying something. Something that took my breath away! Something that, when I saw it last, was in a museum in Berlin. An exquisite alabaster vase carved in the likeness of the god of the underworld – Osiris!'

'Not the Berlin Whatchamacallit Vase?' said Andy.

'The very one,' said Dame Lobelia.

'Well, so what?' said Josh, a little peevishly. To add to his queasy stomach, he was now beginning to suffer from a headache. 'So what if the old codger has got some old vase?'

'Not some old vase. Some old *stolen* vase.'

'Well, so what? What difference does it make?'

'What difference does it make?' She looked astonished. 'My dear Josh, don't you see? That "old codger", as you call him, is a thief. He's more than a thief, he's an arch-thief. A criminal of international proportions. Somewhere he's got a hidden hoard of Egyptian artefacts – treasures that he's stolen from the great museums of the world. And it's in that secret hoard that we will more than likely find what we are looking for, I'm sure.'

'But so *what?*' said Josh. 'We've still got to *find* it haven't we? And we don't even know where to start.'

'On the contrary, we know *exactly* where. The key to everything lies in that library. *That* is where we're going to start. And start without delay.'

***

It was a subdued little band of travellers that continued on their way that afternoon. For a while none of them spoke. Each was lost in thought, wondering what might lie ahead.

Eventually, Katie fell asleep, her head lolling to one side, her breathing becoming deep and measured. Andy gazed moodily out of the window and Josh began to feel carsick.

They stopped for tea at Hambden Ash. But no one felt very hungry after such an enormous lunch and Josh seemed more and more unwell. By the time they reached Coomley Heath, dusk had already fallen and the trees loomed darkly against the evening sky. They drove through the village and a couple of miles beyond and suddenly they saw the house.

It rose on a slight hill, grim and fortress-like. Some windows, few and far between, gleamed palely, but generally the place had a forbidding, cheerless air. They stopped at the gate and at last the lodge-keeper, an evil-looking fellow with a black patch across one eye, came out and let them through.

The drive in front of them curved sharply to the left then dipped. Trees came crowding in from either side and the house soon disappeared from view. Now there was nothing but the winding ribbon of road and the thickening woods.

A sudden downpour made puddles that shone brightly in the headlights and reflected eerie shadows from the branches overhead.

Still the drive snaked on. The trees seemed to be moving closer to the road now. Every so often they reached out suddenly from the darkness and tapped loudly on the roof of the car or brushed against its windows.

'I don't like this drive. When will we be there?'

'Soon, Katie. Very soon.'

But still the drive went on, twisting and turning like a serpent through the dark trees. The rain beat even harder. The wipers dragged uselessly across the windscreen so that the road ahead became almost invisible. The little car slowed to a snail's pace.

Then they started gently climbing. Up from the shallow wooded valley. Out into the open. With a suddenness that made the children catch their breath, the

111

trees abruptly parted. The drive fanned out into a great, gravelled courtyard and the house rose massively in front of them.

Josh gazed uneasily up at its looming battlements. He had a distinctly itchy feeling in his armpits.

Chapter 18

Someone was waiting for them at the servants'
entrance when they drew up. The tall, gaunt, very
upright figure of a man stood silhouetted in the
doorway. He opened a huge, black umbrella and came
down the steps to meet them. As he got nearer the
children saw that he had a pale, skull-like face and dark,
deep-set eyes.

'Why, Mr Mortlock, this *is* an honour,' said Dame
Lobelia with a wry smile and just the faintest hint of
mockery in her tone.

'The lodge-keeper telephoned to say that you were on
your way. In view of the rain I thought that you might be
in need of some assistance.' His voice was cold and
lifeless, his face expressionless, save for the intense look
in his eyes, which glittered like polished jet.

He lifted the largest rucksack from the boot and
carried it up the steps, which was a relief to Josh because
he suddenly felt dead-tired.

They found themselves standing in a dimly lit, stone
passageway somewhere at the back of the house. At the
far end there was a flight of narrow, wooden stairs. To the
right was an oak-beamed, whitewashed kitchen and next
to that, what must once have been the laundry. It had a
row of old-fashioned, stone sinks with brass taps and a

mangle. There were other doors leading to other passages and rooms and perhaps to closets and pantries and larders.

This place is like a rabbit warren, thought Josh.

'Beds have been made up in the room next to yours, Mrs Smith. I have put by something cold for your supper.' He spoke in the same dreary monotone as before.

Dame Lobelia thanked him cheerfully and introduced her 'grandchildren'.

'Children, this is Mr Mortlock. He's the butler here and a very important person at Sedgewick Hall.'

'How do you do?' they murmured. But he ignored the greeting, resting his glittering gaze upon them for only a moment, before turning once again to Dame Lobelia.

'Sir Sebastian has left particular instructions,' he said solemnly, 'that the young persons are to keep strictly to the servants' quarters.'

He spoke the words: 'young persons' with an obvious distaste, as though describing some unpleasant smell.

'Under no circumstances are they to be allowed into the main part of the house, Mrs Smith, on account of the artefacts and works of art.'

'I see.' She was suddenly tight-lipped. 'Sir Sebastian did not mention this to me. The children *will* be disappointed – won't you children?'

They nodded dutifully.

'I've told them so much about the great banqueting hall and the minstrels' gallery and so forth and they were *so* looking forward to seeing it all. Weren't you children?'

Cue for more nodding.

'These are the master's wishes, Mrs Smith. I merely carry out his orders.'

'You do indeed, Mr Mortlock. And most efficiently too, if I may say so.' She gave him an ingratiating smile, which he did not return. 'But don't you think that, just this once, an exception could be made? I mean, what harm would it do if – under the scrutiny of your eagle eye of course – the children were to take a little peek?'

'I'm afraid that would be quite impossible.'

'Well, that's a pity, because you know what children are. The more they're told they cannot do a thing, the more they want to do it. It would be so unfortunate if tomorrow, while I'm busy with my duties, they should be tempted to stray somewhere they shouldn't and then should go and *break* something...' She trailed off, watching him closely. But his face was like a mask, betraying nothing.

'Seeing as he left us *both* in charge,' she went on. 'I think that Sir Sebastian might be inclined to blame *you* as much as me.'

This time she was sure that she saw a flicker of concern in his dark eyes. He seemed to hesitate.

'Well, perhaps there'd be no harm...' he said at length. 'Perhaps there'd be no harm in showing the young persons something of the Hall, especially since the rest of the staff are away for the weekend. But just this once, you understand, just to satisfy their curiosity...'

'Oh, of course, Mr Mortlock. Just this once.'

'Very well then, follow me if you please, and remember...' he turned to the children, his voice almost a hiss, 'don't touch *anything!*'

They trouped along in single file with the butler at their head and Dame Lobelia bringing up the rear. They climbed the narrow stairs at the end of the passageway and turned left along a panelled corridor, passing through a door, studded with iron nails, which creaked noisily on its ancient hinges. After several more twists and turns they went along another passage and down a further flight of stairs until at last, at the end of a long, stone-flagged corridor, they came to an arched door. This, the butler opened and they stepped into a huge, dark space.

All was silent except for the constant drumming of the rain. A sudden flash of lightning lit up tall casement windows and cast strange, gigantic shadows.

A moment later Mortlock flicked some switches and they were dazzled. Light refracted through a thousand twinkling icicles of glass. They were standing in the Great Banqueting Hall under a giant chandelier.

Portraits of Sir Sebastian's ancestors glared at them from every wall. Suits of armour stood sentinel in the corners. At one end there was a huge stone fireplace with fire irons and brassware ranged about it. Above it was a tapestry, embroidered with the Sedgewick coat of arms and scores of human eyes, which seemed to follow them around the room.

The butler went droning on and on, pointing out this and that. A pair of giant Chinese vases, big enough to hide a man inside. A display of swords on the wall, arranged to look like the petals of an enormous flower. Some grinning cherubs' heads moulded out of plaster on the ceiling.

They didn't take much in. His sea of words washed over them like the receding tide over a beach, leaving hardly any mark upon their minds. Tiredness was beginning to catch up with them. It was all that they could manage just to stifle their yawns.

They were making their weary way towards the long gallery at the far end of the hall, hoping desperately that this would be the very last room that they would have to visit, when they passed a finely carved oak door. On a sudden impulse Josh said: 'What's in there?'

'In there?' Mortlock seemed to hesitate. 'That's the library.'

'Can we go in?' said Josh, his hand already trying the handle. But it was locked.

'Sir Sebastian does not like anyone to go in there when he's away. Some of the books are very valuable.'

'We wouldn't touch anything,' said Josh. Some power beyond his will seemed to be urging him on.

'Does the key hang with the others in the closet by the kitchen?' said Dame Lobelia. 'I could go and fetch it.'

'No, I have it here,' the butler said, extracting with obvious reluctance a large key from his waistcoat. In a moment he had turned it in the lock and they had passed inside.

It was a deep, shadowy room and smelt stale and musty. Dark, wood panels and old, leather-bound books lined the walls up to the ceiling and there were heavy curtains at the windows, giving it a closed-in, airless feeling.

On a small table in a gloomy alcove stood a vase of wilting flowers, the petals dropping even as they watched. Dame Lobelia went over to have a look.

'I changed these only yesterday,' she murmured. 'It's really very odd. Nothing seems to survive in here for very long.'

'It smells,' said Katie, wrinkling her nose in disgust. 'Like dead things.'

The murky water in the crystal vase was giving off a faintly fetid smell. It reminded Josh of something.

He went over to the shelves on the far wall, feeling forced, somehow, to go there. He scanned the books, looking for something – he didn't know quite what – and then he felt a violent throbbing pain. He put his hands up to his temples. The headache he'd been nursing since lunchtime had suddenly grown much worse. Little waves of dizziness and nausea swept over him. But still he scanned the shelves. He felt he had to. A voice inside his head was telling him to. It's here, said the voice, it's here, here, on these shelves. And he knew that he was near, so very, very near…

The others saw it first. Katie screamed behind him and someone – Andy – grabbed his arm and violently yanked him back.

'Watch out! Don't step on it! Watch…OUT!'

He looked down at the floor in front of him and yelped. Close to the lowest shelf of books, eyes staring blankly, back broken by the powerful spring of the trap, lay a heap of spiky fur and bloody entrails… a huge, dead rat.

Chapter 19

'Well, you've certainly got to hand it to that man,' said Dame Lobelia, helping herself to more slices of cold chicken and yet another dollop of potato salad. 'There's not much he won't do to keep intruders out of that precious library of his.' She chuckled. 'But it'll take more than a squashed rat to frighten us away. Won't it my young friends?'

The boys smiled weakly. They were in her private sitting room at the top of the great house, balancing their supper plates on their knees and sipping mugs of hot, sweet tea.

Katie had long since gone to bed. After barely a couple of bites of supper she had started rubbing her eyes and yawning constantly. Dame Lobelia had taken her by the hand and led her off to the room next door. It was furnished with three old-fashioned iron bedsteads. She had crawled gratefully beneath the feather eiderdown on one of them and had instantly fallen asleep.

The boys, too, had been made drowsy by their supper. The snug and cosy feel of the sitting room had only made them worse. The deep and comfortable armchairs, the curtains drawn against the driving rain, the lamps casting a soft, rosy glow – all had made it difficult to stay awake.

But the tea was beginning to revive them and now suddenly they were alert and interested.

'Do you mean that somebody actually went and put it there?' said Andy. *'Deliberately?'*

'What better way to scare off nosy parkers?' Dame Lobelia reached for a plate on the little table next to her. 'There was no trap in there yesterday when I went to change the flowers. But now, the moment Sir Sebastian goes away, we find we've got a plague of rodents on our hands. It all seems too convenient to me. More chicken anyone?'

They shook their heads politely and a grubby-looking bandage that had been tied around Josh's forehead slipped off onto his lap.

'How's that head of yours now, young man? Any better?'

'*Much* better, thanks.'

'Thought it would be. Never fails – that *heka* headache poultice. Two parts honey, one part dried crocodile dung and a little sour milk. Of course, it wouldn't have worked without the incantation…'

'Crocodile dung,' Josh looked appalled. 'You didn't really use…?'

'Alas, no…couldn't get any I'm sorry to say. Not so easy to come by in this part of the world and horse manure doesn't work anywhere near so well.'

Horse manure? Josh quickly brushed the bandage off his lap.

'However, some years ago I came across an excellent substitute and luckily I had some with me – the stems of the crocodile root, *crocodilus scutatus*, a little-known herb that has grown wild in Egypt since ancient times. It's a very effective cure for headaches of all kinds, including the dreaded migraine, which I suffer from myself. Are you still feeling sick?'

'No, but I get a bit dizzy when I stand up suddenly.'

'I can't help much with that, I'm afraid,' she said. 'The air around you is disturbed, all stirred up and agitated.'

She leaned towards him, lowering her voice. 'Things may soon start flying about again.'

'Oh no!' said Josh. 'Not that!'

She nodded. 'The amulets are gathering power, you see, now that they're so close, and so the curse is getting stronger.'

She reached into the folds of her capacious skirt and from a cunningly concealed pocket drew out a pouch from which she extracted something. She held out her open hand for them to see. In the cradle of her palm the arc of polished stone seemed to glow with a gently pulsating, violet light.

'That's a sign the other one isn't far away,' she said. 'Once we join them together and say the incantation you'll be safe. But, until then, the closer they get, the more danger you'll be in.'

She sighed. 'And the worst of it is the charms you're wearing will be getting weaker by the hour.'

'What do you mean?' said Josh. His hand flew to his throat. 'You don't mean they're going to stop protecting me?'

'Not altogether, Josh, I hope. But I'll be frank with you.' She looked him squarely in the eyes. 'It just might come to that. We're dealing with powerful magic here, my friend. Tomb curses are the hardest ones to lift. That's why we can't delay. Why we've got to act tomorrow – or tomorrow night, to be precise.'

'But how?' asked Andy. 'We can't go *near* the library, let alone *inside* it.'

'That's why I said tomorrow *night*...' Somewhere, deep within the house, a clock was chiming midnight. '...At around about this time, in fact. With Mortlock safely tucked up in bed and nobody there to see us – *that's* when we'll make our move.'

She stifled a yawn. 'Time for bed, my friends,' she said, wearily stacking their empty plates on the little table beside her. 'We've got a busy night ahead of us tomorrow.'

They made their way out into the shadowy passage. The rain had stopped and a brilliant moon lit up the mullioned window by the stairs.

'Josh, take these,' she said softly, handing him a little, leather, drawstring pouch. 'Put them around your pillow tonight...just in case.'

In the bedroom, he emptied the little bag into his palm. Gleaming palely in the moonlight was what looked like a clutch of tiny dragon's teeth. They were six small cloves of garlic.

***

It was about two a.m. when he suddenly awoke feeling terribly afraid. He lay staring up into the darkness and listening to the pounding of his heart. He couldn't move a muscle. *There was something on his bed.*

Something about the size of a large cat was squatting near his legs. He could feel its compact weight pulling the covers taut across his knees.

But he knew it was no cat. Nor dog for that matter. Nor any other cuddly, furry creature. He knew – even before he caught a whiff of its stinking, putrid breath – that he was in the presence of something inexpressibly malevolent and evil.

It moved slightly. And then it moved again, advancing from side to side in a series of small, sudden jerks towards his chest.

He wanted to cry out but the scream stayed, strangled, in his throat. There was cold sweat on his forehead and he thought his heart was going to burst with fear.

He squeezed his eyes tightly shut. Now the thing was right on top of him. He could feel its breath directly on his face. Little monkey claws fumbled horribly around his neck. It was trying to unknot the rope of charms. This is it, thought Josh, I'm going to die. Silently, like an insect, without even uttering a sound.

But then there was a sound: a dreadful hiss of rage and pain. The creature leapt up and landed on the floor. The pungent smell of garlic filled the air.

Josh felt his muscles suddenly unlock. He struggled up in bed and opened terrified eyes. But whatever it was, it was in retreat. It scuttled, towards the farthest shadowy corner of the room. There seemed to be a hole there in the skirting. It turned for a second and Josh saw a single fiery eye stare directly at him with what he sensed was utter hatred. Then, in another moment it was gone.

He shrank back beneath the covers of his bed. He lay there trembling for quite a while, listening to the rhythmic breathing of the others and wishing he could wake them up. Neither of them had even stirred. He thought about calling out to Andy, but Katie's bed was between them and he didn't want to disturb her. The idea of getting up and padding over in the dark to shake him was far too frightening to contemplate.

So he just lay there, shivering. Later, much later, when exhaustion finally overwhelmed him, he sank into a fitful sleep.

Chapter 20

Everyone was late for breakfast, including Dame Lobelia, who was never late for anything. But this morning she had hit the snooze button twice and still had not been able to get up. On the third attempt she had finally managed to haul herself out of bed.

'It's really most unusual for me,' she said, pouring herself an extra-strong cup of coffee. 'I never oversleep. I always make a particular point of rising early to embrace the day.'

And it certainly was a day well worth embracing. The rain had now completely gone, leaving everything refreshed. And it was gloriously sunny. The cloudless sky held promise of midday heat.

'I've only a few chores to do this morning, children, and a couple of errands to run and then I'll be free. What do you say to a picnic by the lake and then a spot of exploration of the grounds?'

'Yay!'

'Wicked!'

'Can we go exploring on our own this morning?' said Andy.

'If you stay out of the main part of the house, of course you can,' said Dame Lobelia. 'But try to be back by one o'clock. If you fancy going blackberrying there's a mass of bushes beside the path through the woods. You'll find a basket on the floor in the pantry. Oh and Josh...' she added, smiling, 'make sure you keep that football well away from any windows.'

***

Ten minutes later they set off, Katie, with the basket on her arm. The boys dribbled the ball between them as they followed the lane towards the trees and their sister chattered constantly.

'I'm going to pick lots and lots of blackberries and then I'm going to ask Dame...' she broke off with a horrified gasp and clapped her hand over her mouth. Looking furtively about her, she saw that Mortlock had just emerged from behind the house with one of the dogs. '...*Grandma*...' she corrected herself, loudly enough for him to hear, '...I'm going to ask *Grandma* if I can make a pie.'

'We haven't come here to play at cooking,' said Josh. 'We've got more important things to do.'

'Like playing footy,' said Andy, doing kick-ups with the ball.

'It isn't playing at cooking. That's what babies do with play-dough. It's proper cooking.'

'Yours isn't.'

Katie scowled and seeing that Andy appeared to be smirking, she turned her fire on him.

'Anyway, football isn't important. It's just a stupid game.'

Instead of rising to the bait, he flipped the ball backwards over his head and grinned good-naturedly at her.

'Well, something happened to me last night that really was important,' said Josh, 'while you lot were asleep.'

He had been itching to tell them about the dreadful visitation all through breakfast, but the presence of the ever-watchful butler had prevented him. Now that they were out of earshot of the house he could do it.

'What do you mean: "while we were asleep"?'

Andy had stopped playing with the ball and there was an expression of wide-eyed interest on Katie's face.

'You two snored through the whole thing.'

'*I* don't snore!' protested Katie. Then, remembering she was a Brownie, she added truthfully, 'Well, only sometimes, when I've got a cold.'

'What "whole thing"?' said Andy. 'What are you talking about?'

After a dramatically pregnant pause Josh told them what had happened in the night. They listened with rapt attention as he described in graphic detail the creature's awful smell, the horrible feel of its little hands upon his neck, its dreadful, inhuman hiss and piercing fiery eye.

When he had finished, there was a gratifyingly stunned silence. It was Andy who broke it. He said something that he instantly regretted. 'Are you sure you didn't dream it?'

Josh stared at him ashen-faced and no one moved. His fists were clenched so that the nails dug deep crescents in his palms. Katie bit her lip. It looked like Josh might hit him.

'How can you *dare* say that?' he spat. 'After everything that's happened!'

Andy, all colour drained now from his face, opened his mouth to speak. Instead there came a loud and plaintive bleat. A sheep in a nearby field had been

127

watching them, unblinking, through the barbed wire fence, chewing all the while. They turned to meet its gaze and it bleated again, as if in mournful agreement.

Katie giggled, the tension evaporated and everybody laughed.

'Well, at least the sheep believes me, anyway.'

'Sorry bruv,' said Andy, looking thoroughly ashamed. 'I don't know how I could have said that. Sometimes I just want to pretend this isn't happening I suppose.'

'Well, how do you think *I* feel?' said Josh.

They walked on in silence for a while and joined a dry-mud track that branched off to the right. It wound around the edge of a small field and through an opening in the trees. They followed it with the sense that something pleasurable was coming and within a few short minutes they had stashed the football by a stile and plunged into the woods.

The trees grew close together and a carpet of bracken and ferns covered what space there was in-between. Dead leaves and broken twigs crackled noisily under their feet and their voices sounded unnaturally loud. It seemed to them that they were intruders in this cool and dappled world.

They came upon the wild blackberries just as Dame Lobelia had said. They grew densely beside the narrow path, choking it in places with their prickly, trailing stems.

The fruit was large and luscious and they picked it eagerly, shovelling as much into their mouths as they put into their basket. But the best and biggest were always just out of reach and they found themselves straying further and further from the track.

Eventually, with basket and bellies full of blackberries, they turned once more towards the path. They went this way and that, but they couldn't seem to find it. For fifteen minutes or more they searched without success until, at last, they reached a sunny clearing and realised that they were well and truly lost.

They sat down on a huge fallen tree trunk to consider what to do. Next to it was the splintered stump from which it had been severed, probably by lightning. It had been a giant in its day, perhaps some thirty metres high.

'Let's keep quiet and listen,' said Andy. 'Maybe we'll be able to hear the sound of traffic.'

But there was nothing, just birdsong and a faint mechanical hum, far too distant to be useful.

'Why don't we shout for help?' suggested Katie. 'Maybe someone will come and rescue us.'

'That's a brilliant idea,' said Josh, 'considering we're in the middle of a wood and nowhere near a house or road.'

'Well, have you got a better one then, clever clogs?'

'If we climbed a tree we'd be able to see which direction we should head in.'

They looked about them for trees that were easy to climb and tall enough to give them a view over the others.

'If you give me a leg up, I think I could climb that one.' Josh pointed towards a gnarled old oak that stood on a bank surrounded by brambles and nettles.

'I think it should be the other way around,' said Andy. 'You're heavier than me.'

'Okay, whatever you like, but let's get on with it. It's gone twelve, already and we've got to get back.'

The boys waded through the brambles and clambered up the bank. Andy scoured the lower branches looking for one that he could reach. He made his way behind the massive trunk and disappeared from sight.

The others never saw him slip. They only heard his frightened cry echoing up, as though from somewhere underground. And then, a moment later, when Josh reached the spot, he seemed to have completely vanished.

Chapter 21

'**A**ndy! Andy! Where are you?'
'Down here!'
'Down where?'
'Down *here!*'

Josh took a cautious step in the direction of the voice. It seemed to be coming from the roots of the great oak.

A sudden shriek distracted him. Katie, struggling through the brambles with her basket, had tripped, spilling half its contents into the undergrowth. He went over and helped her up, guiding her towards the bank.

'What's happened?' she said. 'Where's Andy?'

'He's fallen down a hole.'

'*It's not a hole.*' A disembodied head was poking up out of the ground, amongst the ferns. The rest of Andy soon followed. There were dark stains on his T-shirt and bits of bark and dead leaves in his hair. 'There are steps!' he said, '…and a tunnel. Come and look!'

He parted the tangled foliage to reveal a mossy stone stairway that descended steeply into dank shadow.

'Let's see where it goes,' said Josh.

Katie hung back. 'It's dark down there.'

'I've got my torch,' said Andy switching on the pocket flashlight that he always carried, along with a penknife, clipped to the belt of his jeans.

'Well, *I'm* going, anyway,' said Josh. 'You can stay up here if you like.'

'Not on my own.'

'You'll have to come then, won't you?'

'Be careful it's slippery,' said Andy, leading the way.

Inside it smelt of damp and mildew and the rough stone walls felt slimy to the touch. At the bottom they stood on a floor of wet gravel and Andy shone his torch for them to see. The ground sloped gently downwards and the tunnel disappeared into pitch darkness.

They started along it, their feet making a noisy, crunching sound. The torchlight cast huge shadows on the walls behind them. Once or twice Katie glanced back at the thin shaft of daylight on the steps. It grew fainter by the second. Then they rounded a sharp bend and it had gone. Before and behind them was nothing but impenetrable blackness.

They walked on for almost fifteen minutes, twisting and turning so often that they lost all sense of direction. Water dripped from the roof onto their heads and once something – he felt sure it was a bat – brushed Josh's head lightly as it flew by. He gave a cry of fright that echoed strangely up and down the tunnel.

'It can't go on much longer,' he said. 'What's the point of it? It must end soon.'

The little torch was beginning to fail. Its gleam had become a feeble orange glow. Suddenly it died.

They stood in total darkness, groping for each other's hands. Katie whimpered.

'It's all right Katie,' said Andy, with a confidence he didn't really feel. 'If we hold hands and touch the walls as we go, we can keep up a decent pace. We'll be out in no time.'

'I don't want to touch the walls,' said Katie, her voice small and trembling on the verge of tears. 'They're slimy.'

'It's okay, you won't have to,' said Andy. 'We'll put you in the middle and you can hold our hands.'

'Who's bright idea was it to come down here, anyway?' said Josh.

'Yours!' reminded Katie.

They struggled on, in total darkness, groping their way along the dripping walls, for what seemed like an eternity of time. No one spoke. The only sound was the echoing crunch of their feet upon the gravel and – in their heads – the wild beating of their hearts.

At last they appeared to be gently climbing.

'We *must* be getting near the exit now,' said Andy.

Josh halted suddenly. 'Perhaps there is no exit. Perhaps it's a dead end.' He had been fighting off a rising sense of panic for several minutes. 'I think we should go back.'

'Are you crazy?' said Andy. 'After we've come all this way?'

'No… I really think we should…' He tugged at the rope of charms around his neck as if it was a too-tight collar. He couldn't breathe. There was a tight, squeezing feeling in his chest.

'This could go on for miles…I'm going back…'

He turned abruptly and then let out a gasp of terror. Behind him in the distance there was something. A tiny glowing point of light. It wasn't daylight.

The others saw it too. It seemed to be advancing, almost imperceptibly, from side to side. For a moment they were rooted to the spot. Then Andy grabbed the others' hands: 'Come on!'

He yanked them hard and they stumbled forwards, whimpering with fear, their hands skimming the dripping walls. They swung around a bend and then another and then suddenly ahead they saw a trace of daylight.

They hit the bottom step running. The next moment they were clambering upwards, their arms reaching to part the overhanging branches in front of them. Then, with a final surge of effort, they burst through into the daylight and fresh air.

They stood there panting – half with terror, half with relief – in a small sun-dappled copse.

'Do you think it'll come up after us?' said Katie.

Behind them there was a sudden rustle in the undergrowth. They nearly jumped out of their skins. A startled rabbit darted out in front of them towards the margin of the trees.

They moved as one, crashing through the bushes after it. A moment later they were fully out, in the open of a sunny field, beside a narrow lane. There was some rusty farm machinery and a disused barn nearby and beyond them was a high, stone wall.

'Where the heck are we?' panted Josh.

'Outside,' said Andy, peering up at something on the wall.

'Brilliant! But *where* outside exactly?'

'Outside the grounds of Sedgewick Hall. We've come right underneath the wall. Look!' He pointed up at something carved into the stonework. A shield, bearing six human eyes and supported by two griffins: the Sedgewick coat of arms.

'A secret way out!' exclaimed Josh.

'Or in,' said Andy.

'Speaking of which – how *do* we get back in?'

'Follow the wall round to the lodge-keeper's gate, I suppose, and ring the bell.'

'Uh, huh?' Josh folded his arms and tilted his head quizzically to one side. 'And what, exactly, do we say when he asks us how we got out in the first place?'

'Oh,' said Andy. 'I see what you mean.'

'Well, I'm not going down that tunnel again, not for anything,' said Katie.

'No.' Josh shivered despite the noonday sun.

'If we keep to the wall we might find some other way in – a gap perhaps or a gate that isn't locked.' Andy glanced at his watch. 'It's gone half-past twelve. We've got less than thirty minutes. Come on, let's start walking!'

***

There was no gap or unlocked gate. The wall just seemed to go on forever. Huge and solid and far too steep to climb. They plodded through the midday heat feeling increasingly worried. Nothing passed them on the quiet road. Once, up ahead there was a fox, which loped unhurriedly into a thicket when it saw them.

It was almost too late before they heard the car. It came roaring around a blind bend hooting furiously and, narrowly missing them, careered into a hedge.

They knew, even before they saw its driver get out and come towards them, that there was something very familiar about it. It was Dame Lobelia's Morris Minor.

***

The journey back through the lodge gates was an uncomfortable one for the three of them, huddled hotly under the heavy tartan travel-rug that Dame Lobelia always carried in her car. But it worked because the lodge-keeper never noticed they were there.

When they reached the seclusion of the trees the old lady stopped the car and told them to walk the rest of the way back to the Hall, to make it look as though they had been no further than the woods. They were, she said, to go straight up to their bedroom and quietly pack their things and wait for her.

'But we've just *un*packed,' said Katie, who had finished neatly filling the drawers of her bedside table only that morning. Her Tiny Teddy, her hairbrush and the contents of the little vanity bag she'd got for Christmas (including the dregs of a bottle of cologne she'd pinched off Mum) had all been carefully arranged on the table-top beside her. Now Dame Lobelia was saying that she had to pack it all up again. It was really most annoying.

'I know dear, but it's best to be prepared,' said Dame Lobelia.

'For what?' said Josh.

'For every eventuality, my young friend. This discovery of yours this morning has put an entirely different complexion on things. Let's just say that we might need to make a sudden getaway, that's all.'

'But why…?'

Dame Lobelia would brook no more questions. 'I'll see you there in half an hour; make sure that you don't dawdle.' And she roared off up the drive.

***

True to her word, thirty minutes later, she appeared, flushed with the effort of having dragged an enormous, wicker picnic-hamper up three flights of stairs. The children, who had been having tummy rumbles for quite a while, were more than pleased to see it. But when she lifted up the lid it revealed, not the tempting array of sandwiches and cakes they had expected, but a gaping void.

'Put your bags in here, children, and strap it shut. You two boys can carry it down the stairs.'

'But why…?' Josh began.

'We've got to get these bags out to the car without it being noticed my dear Josh. And Mortlock's on the prowl. Do you see?'

'I suppose so, but…'

Katie's stomach interrupted the proceedings. It gurgled loudly like an old radiator.

'I'm starving, where's the picnic?' she said.

'In the first-aid box in the car,' said Dame Lobelia in a matter-of-fact sort of way. As if that was just where you'd expect to find it.

They drove down to the lake and had their picnic. Dame Lobelia questioned them closely concerning the whereabouts of the secret tunnel they had found. When they described the great lightning-struck tree trunk they had sat on, she knew the place at once.

After a long and leisurely lunch she left them to their own devices for the afternoon, saying that she had to drive into the village on a final errand. They whiled away their time paddling in the lake trying to catch tiddlers in a beaker. And climbing trees and lying in the grass. And Katie made a chain of buttercups and daisies.

It was getting on for six o'clock when they made their way back up towards the house. The sun was getting lower in the sky, but it was still pleasantly warm. The ever-watchful eye of Mortlock was upon them as they shuffled up the drive. He had just been around the back to feed the guard-dogs.

They noticed with mild concern that the Morris Minor wasn't in its usual parking space. They were just thinking that Dame Lobelia was rather late when they heard the sound of wheels behind them. Light wheels that skimmed the gravel. The children turned to look and saw a portly figure on a bicycle, red-faced and peddling furiously. They waited until she had caught them up and spoke almost with a single voice.

'What's happened to the car?'

She looked beyond them to the steps where Mortlock loitered, waiting for her answer.

'Broken down,' she said breathlessly. 'Left it in a lay-by near the village. The carburettor's gone kaput!'

Chapter 22

It was well after midnight when the little group assembled in the passageway outside the children's bedroom.

'Is everybody ready?' whispered Dame Lobelia. 'Got your torches?'

The children nodded.

'And the pepper?'

'Yes.'

'Excellent! Now follow me!'

They tiptoed down a series of dark corridors and numerous flights of narrow stairs, wincing at every creak and groan the old house made. Once, when they thought that they heard footsteps above them on a landing, they stopped to listen. But there was no one there.

They paused nervously for a moment, before crossing the moonlit hall towards the library. Eyes seemed to be watching them from the portraits on the walls.

The carved oak door was locked. At their unspoken question Dame Lobelia pressed her finger to her lips. She drew out a key from her pocket, turned it quietly in the lock and they slipped inside.

'What happens now?' said Andy.

'That depends on Josh,' said Dame Lobelia. 'This room holds the key to what we're seeking, but it's Josh who has to find it.'

'Me? Why me? I don't know any more than you do.'

'Don't be afraid,' soothed Dame Lobelia. 'Just let your sixth sense guide you as it did last night. And remember, Josh, you're not alone. We're with you.'

'Yeah, we're right behind you, bruv,' said Andy, patting him on the back.

They moved deeper into the room and Katie shone her flashlight on the flowers in the alcove. 'They're completely dead, now,' she murmured. Their shrivelled petals and dry, curling leaves cast tall, contorted shadows on the wall behind them.

'It would help if we had some idea of what we were looking for,' said Andy.

'A door,' said Josh suddenly. 'We're looking for a door...' He broke off, perplexed. 'I don't know why I said that...'

'There's only one door here as far as I can see,' said Andy, 'and that's the one we came through.'

But Josh was already making his way towards the shelves on the far wall, just as he had done the night before. There were hundreds of books there, of every size and thickness and he scanned them feverishly... *Myth, Magic and Mayhem in Ancient Egypt; Pyramid Power and the Evil Eye; Secrets of Sarcophagi...* He swept his flashlight along them, row by row... *Pharaohs' Funerals; Death's Door and the Journey to the Afterlife; Problems with Papyri...* He paused and went back to the previous volume. It sat plumply on the bottom shelf, shabby in its torn and faded dustcover. He wouldn't have given it a second glance had it not been for the name of the author on its spine. 'There's one of your books here.'

Dame Lobelia went over. 'Ah yes… *Death's Door*…' she murmured. 'An early work and not my best by any means.'

'It's a bit battered though,' said Josh, picking up the chunky volume, whereupon its cover immediately fell off and several of its pages fluttered to the floor.

'It's certainly been well thumbed,' she agreed. 'I suppose I should feel flattered.'

Josh bent down to put it back and then he stopped.

'Hey, there's something in here.'

He was peering into the gap from which the book had been removed. He reached between two leather-bound tomes, feeling for something at the back. It was a lever or a handle of some kind. He grasped it, but no sooner had he done so than he leapt backwards with a cry of shock.

The wall had suddenly begun to move. Silently and smoothly the entire wall of books was swinging open like a giant door. Through its cavernous mouth they could see a flight of steps and beyond that, a sloping passageway tunnelling into inky darkness.

A rush of stale, fusty air came up to meet them as they stood there, for a moment, gathering their wits and summoning up their courage.

Then Dame Lobelia spoke. 'Well, this is it, my young friends.' She took a deep breath. 'Shall we go?'

Josh had barely started down the steps when he suddenly pulled back. For no apparent reason he had begun to shake from head to foot. He felt a tightening, squeezing feeling in his chest that made it hard to breathe. 'I can't!'

Dame Lobelia came back up and gripped him firmly by the arm. 'You've got to, Josh!'

He stubbornly shook his head.

'Josh, I understand how frightened you are. I really do. But you've got to carry on!'

He didn't speak. He couldn't. But his eyes betrayed his panic.

'You've got to, Josh!' urged Andy. 'You've got to! We're almost there for goodness sake!'

'Yes,' said Katie, 'you can't give up now...'

'Josh' said Dame Lobelia slowly, 'you owe it to yourself and to rest of us to see this business through.'

He hesitated, scanning their anxious faces. Then he swallowed hard. 'All right.'

'Good man.' She patted him on the shoulder. 'Now, come on!'

Cautiously, they made their way down the steps, then down a steeply sloping passageway, then down another flight of steps. Deeper and deeper, under the foundations of the great house. No one spoke. Only their echoing footsteps broke the silence.

When, at last, the floor appeared to level out and it seemed that they could go no deeper, they came to yet another flight of steps. At its foot they paused, aware that they were on the edge of a great space. They shone their torches upwards and the sight that met their eyes made them catch their breath in wonder.

The tunnel had fanned out into a high, broad chamber, whose star-studded ceiling was supported by six brightly-painted columns. Pictures of gods and goddesses, birds and animals – all manner of exotic creatures – adorned every surface, so that the whole room gleamed in the torchlight like a many-faceted jewel. In every nook and cranny there were artefacts and at the far end, in a recess in the wall, there stood a great stone statue of Osiris.

'It's like a tomb,' breathed Katie, who recalled seeing a picture of something very similar in *Mysterious Mummies.*

'It *is* a tomb,' murmured Dame Lobelia. She shone her torch on something in the centre. A huge granite sarcophagus, crowded with carvings, sat open on a raised platform. Its shadow loomed, immense, behind it.

'There isn't anything in it, though,' said Katie. 'Is there?'

'Let's go and see.' Dame Lobelia strode purposefully towards the great stone box and resting her hands on its rim, raised herself on tiptoes to look inside.

A pair of darkly gleaming, human eyes stared up at her out of a face of burnished gold. She gasped – the Karnak Mask! So she'd been right – it *had* been Sedgewick who had taken it.

The mask covered the head and most of the shoulders of the mummy, which lay in an open wooden coffin with its arms crossed on its breast. One blackened, bony finger protruded where the bandages had come away. It seemed to point at her, accusingly.

And there was something more... Something that made her heart almost miss a beat. Glowing beneath one of the mummy's bandaged hands was a curve of gently pulsating, violet light...

'Can you reach it?' she whispered to Josh, who was standing by her side, transfixed. 'My arms aren't long enough.'

He didn't speak. His mouth was dry and he felt deathly sick. The putrid smell of rotting meat filled his nostrils and that tight feeling in his chest had come back. He put his hand up to his throat and shook his head.

'But Josh you must! No one else is tall enough. It must be you!'

He stood hesitating, trying to will himself to do it.

'Someone's coming! Look!' cried Andy.

At the far end of the chamber, beside the statue, two beams of light from torches swept the walls and floor of a passageway that they had not noticed was there.

'Quick!' hissed Dame Lobelia. 'Get it!'

But Josh didn't move.

Andy made a leap at the sarcophagus, trying desperately to haul himself onto its rim. But it was no good, he wasn't tall enough.

Now there was the sound of footsteps rapidly approaching.

'Josh! This is your last chance! They're almost here!' Dame Lobelia shook him by the shoulders.

'Oh Josh, go on! Go on!' urged Katie. 'They're coming! They're coming!'

Maybe it was the sight of his brother's frantic efforts to save him or his little sister's terror or maybe it was the old lady's words, but something clicked in Josh's brain. As if awoken from a trance he launched himself at the sarcophagus, hauled himself onto its rim and reached right down inside.

It seemed to him that he spent hours fumbling with those dead fingers, desperately trying to prize the amulet from their grip. But it was only a matter of seconds. When, at last, he had it. He swung back up exhausted and stumbled off the platform. The old lady grabbed the shining arc of stone from his weakening grasp and quickly mounted the stone steps beside the sarcophagus.

'Asir neb Djedu netcher aha neb Abdju – Osiris lord of Djedu, great god, lord of Adydos – cut the ties that bind him! The crocodile in the water and the snake upon the land! Release your erring servant from this curse!'

Her voice rang echoing through the chamber as she held the amulets together above his head. There was a sudden flash of light as they fused into a perfect circle and then he fell, fainting, to the floor.

Chapter 23

'Well, well, well…what have we here?' The voice from the far end of the chamber was coldly mocking. '*Tomb-robbers,* no less.'

Feeling as though a heavy weight had suddenly been lifted from his shoulders, Josh struggled up. He stood with the others, squinting in the torch glare.

Someone must have flicked a switch, for the huge room was all at once bathed in a dim yellowish light and they were able to make out the figures of two men. One, tall and gaunt, the children recognised instantly as the butler, Mortlock. He had two fierce-looking dogs on short, chain leashes. The other, a smaller, slightly-built man, they had never seen before.

Dame Lobelia drew herself up to her full five feet, one and three quarter inches and looked the speaker in the eye.

'On the contrary, Sir Sebastian, we are recovering stolen property.'

Now that he was no more than a few steps away, they had a clear view of his weasel features and his brush moustache and close-set, steel-grey eyes.

'You think you're very clever, don't you? You and your so-called "grandchildren"…' He fixed them with a stare of icy contempt. 'But you haven't been quite clever enough... *Dame Lobelia Carter-Smythe...*'

Dame Lobelia gave a slight start.

'Oh yes, I know who you are,' he sneered. 'I saw through your pathetic little deception almost from the first.'

She said nothing. Unseen by anyone, she had slipped her hand into her pocket and was discreetly searching for something.

'Your reputation, you see, is not unfamiliar to me. On my library shelves I have every book you've ever written. I have read them all. And I might add, without exception, every one of them has proved to be a total waste of time.'

'One wonders why you bothered,' said Dame Lobelia. 'A person of your superior intellect and brain.'

'You're so right about my intellect and brain. There is little someone such as *you* could teach me about ancient Egypt. However, there was *one* thing I thought that I might learn...'

He paused, waiting for a question that she didn't ask.

'Don't you want to know what it is?'

She shrugged. A slight, contemptuous, shrug that said she didn't care.

'Well, never mind,' he said. 'I'll tell you anyway. I was curious, you see, as to the whereabouts of a certain amulet – the twin to one that was recently stolen from the British Museum.'

'You *knew* there was another one?'

Sir Sebastian smiled. 'That surprised you didn't it? You might have managed to fool the world, Dame Lobelia, but you never did fool me. I always suspected that it had a twin. The inscription didn't look quite right to me – unfinished somehow. I made discreet inquiries about it in Egypt and all roads led to you.'

He gave a cold, exultant laugh. 'But never in my wildest dreams did I imagine that you would so obligingly drop it into my lap like this! Without my even having to lift a finger to lay hands upon it!'

He gave her a long look through narrowed, searching eyes. 'I've heard these amulets, when put together, have certain properties,' he said. 'Unusual properties. Properties that might even be described as – not that I give credence to such things of course – as *supernatural*.'

'Superstitious rumours,' said Dame Lobelia, shrugging. 'I wouldn't believe everything you hear.'

'Hmm… perhaps not. But, nonetheless, it makes me want to have them all the more. So now I'll trouble you, if you wouldn't mind, to hand them over.'

'And if I do, what happens then? What happens to us?'

'Not *if* you do, but *when* you do,' he gently corrected her. 'It's not as though you have a choice…' He raised his forearm and she saw that in his hand there was a pistol.

'*When* you do…' he repeated, 'why, then you'll join our friend.' He gestured towards the mummy. 'Do I make myself quite clear?'

There was a brief, horrified silence. Then Katie whimpered. Josh put a comforting arm around her shoulders.

'You can't *kill* us!' he said. 'You'll never get away with it – our parents know we're here! They'll come and look for us! They'll tell the police!'

'*Our parents know we're here! They'll come and look for us!*' Sir Sebastian mimicked in a high-pitched voice. 'What a clever boy you are. I never thought of that.' His features twisted into an ugly mask of hatred and contempt. 'You must think that I'm *stupid!* NO ONE knows you're here! Do you think I haven't made quite sure of that? Do you think I haven't made it absolutely certain that I can cover up my tracks?'

His face relaxed and he continued mildly: 'Your car will be disposed of – somewhere in the sea off Beachy Head I rather think would be a good idea. It will be assumed that your atrocious driving has at last led to a fatal accident – that you have driven off the cliff and that you and your passengers are now food for the fishes. In the unlikely event that you – you foolish old woman – are traced to me, I will merely say that I had no idea of your true identity. I might even add that you did a moonlight flit, taking several of my priceless artefacts with you. Rather a good plan, don't you think? And so very, very simple.'

'I congratulate you,' said Dame Lobelia. 'You seem to have thought of everything.'

'Oh, I *have*,' he said. '*Absolutely* everything. Now, if you please, I'd like the amulets.'

'Even so,' said Dame Lobelia. 'I hardly think that you'd be rash enough to fire a gun in here. A bullet ricocheting off these walls might do some serious damage to these artefacts.'

He gave a small unpleasant smile. 'I see you've caught me out. You're right of course, I wouldn't risk a shot down here. But there are other ways...' He waved the gun at Josh. 'Would you mind moving back a step or two?'

'What for?' said Josh.

'Well, please yourself. Don't say I didn't warn you.' He had walked over to a column on his left and with his free hand was pulling on a small lever hidden in a recess in the stone.

When Josh did decide to move, it was too late. A trap door had opened in the ceiling above his head and something – a heavy coil of rope – fell across his shoulders making him scream out.

Only it wasn't a coil of rope. The warm, smooth, undulating thing was alive. It wound itself in swift, sinuous curves around his throat and chest and began to crush the breath out of his lungs.

'The more you struggle the more he'll squeeze,' said Sir Sebastian. 'I advise you to keep still.' He switched his gaze to Dame Lobelia, 'Now, if you wouldn't mind, the amulets – I'd like them.' He held out his hand.

She looked down at the circle in her palm. Taking a scrap of paper with some writing on it from her pocket, she quickly placed it within the ring of stone and muttered something under her breath. *'Ouroboros, O powerful one! I call upon you! O Snake that bites its tail! Enclose the Named Ones within the circle of your protection!'*

Sir Sebastian moved towards her threateningly. 'I've had enough of this,' he said. 'I warn you, my patience is running out! What in the name of Seth…!'

He stopped in his tracks, transfixed. The gun drooped slowly in his fingers and fell with an echoing clatter onto the dark, stone floor. Something was stirring in the depths of the sarcophagus. Something that reeked of death and putrefaction. For a terrible moment it seemed as though the mummy itself might be rising up before them. Then two small, scaly, claw-like hands appeared gripping the rim of the great stone box and behind them the dome of a dark head. In the centre of its forehead was a single fiery eye.

The snake relaxed its grip and dropped onto the floor. It slithered away into the shadows, out of sight. The dogs, frantic with excitement now, barked furiously and strained wildly at their leads.

Dame Lobelia seized the moment. 'Quick! Out through that tunnel by the statue over there!'

But Josh wasn't moving. He clutched his throat, waiting for the familiar, tight, constricting feeling in his chest.

'It's all right Josh! You're safe now! Safe! Come on!'

'Oh no, you don't!' shouted Sir Sebastian. 'Let the dogs loose!'

Mortlock fumbled to release them and they leapt free as though they were a single animal.

'Not *there* you stupid brutes!' yelled Sir Sebastian. The mass of snapping, snarling teeth and rippling muscle had plunged into the sarcophagus and was struggling with something that spat and hissed and smelt abominable.

'Josh – the tunnel! Quick!' Andy franticly pulled his brother by the arm and the two scrambled after the others towards the gaping passageway at the far end of the chamber.

They were barely nine or ten metres into it when the deafening crack of a pistol-shot rang out behind them. There was a rumble like thunder, then a crash of falling masonry and the whole earth seemed to shake. When they turned and shone their flashlights on the entrance – it wasn't there. Instead, the great stone face of Osiris gazed back at them from amid a sea of rubble.

Chapter 24

'Phew! That was close!' Josh leaned, exhausted, against the tunnel wall and slid down onto his haunches.

'Was it an earthquake or what?' said Andy, gazing, stunned, at the great chunks of granite blocking the passageway behind them. 'It couldn't have been the *gun* could it?'

'It was something rather smaller than a gun,' said Dame Lobelia. 'But infinitely more powerful.'

They turned and stared at her.

'Before we set off tonight I took the precaution of writing all our names on a scrap of paper.'

She held out the amulet in her palm and they saw that within the glowing circle there was a little square of folded paper.

'I remember,' said Katie. 'You told us that if you write your name and put it in the amulet – only you called it something else, I can't remember what…' She faltered.

'The magic knot of *shen*,' Dame Lobelia reminded her.

'Yes, that's it! If you put your name in the magic knot of *shen*, you said, then it protects you forever. But you mustn't break the circle, because if you do all the protection flies away – or something like that...I think you said...'

'I said almost exactly that. Quite right,' said Dame Lobelia. 'And you've brought up a very important point. Hold my torch for me a moment, will you please?'

With her freed hand she extracted a clean, linen handkerchief from her pocket and tied it around the amulet, knotting it securely to keep the circle firmly in place.

That's as safe as houses now,' she said, putting it back into her pocket. 'But we'd better move or they'll be heading us off! Don't forget, they know exactly where this tunnel ends – which is more than we do.'

They hurried onwards and this time it proved to be quite a trek. There were no steep slopes or flights of steps. Instead, a long, gentle upward-incline seemed to meander on forever. After a while, the paving underfoot gave way to a floor of damp gravel. The moist air took on an earthy smell and occasionally a tree root poked out between cracks in the rough stone walls.

When, eventually, they emerged at the far end, they found themselves standing on the edge of a wood, beneath a brilliant moon. Nearby, beside a stile, something in the undergrowth shone, ghostly white. It was the football that the children had stashed that morning.

'Well now, who'd have thought we'd come out here?' exclaimed Dame Lobelia. 'How very cleverly concealed it is.'

But there was no time to loiter, for they could hear the sound of barking in the distance. When they turned to look they saw the flash of torches coming their way.

'Quick!' hissed Dame Lobelia. 'Get out your pepper and follow me!' She was already climbing over the stile into the fastness of the wood. 'Sprinkle it behind you as you go – HURRY!'

Without a backward glance, Katie and Andy did as they were told and Josh, pausing only to pocket his torch and scoop up his football, clambered after them.

They were well into the thick of the trees when the barking suddenly tailed off.

'That'll keep 'em off the scent,' grinned Dame Lobelia, brandishing her pepper pot with a chuckle. 'Now, we've got to find this tunnel of yours. I've an idea it's not too far…'

They plodded on through the darkness, all the while straining their ears for sounds of their pursuers.

'Here's where the blackberries start,' said Dame Lobelia, shining her torch on a clump of bushes. 'Not far beyond this point we've got to leave the path and veer off to the left.'

But after they had walked on for ten more minutes they arrived at a fork and Dame Lobelia came to an abrupt halt.

'I have to admit that I've absolutely no idea where we are,' she said.

'Do you mean to say we're lost?' said Josh. 'I thought you said you knew the place?'

'I'd know it in the daylight. But somehow things don't look quite the same at night. We could have overshot it, I suppose.'

'But if we go back,' said Katie, casting an anxious glance over her shoulder, 'they might catch up with us.'

'Shhh!' interrupted Andy. 'I think I hear something.'

They listened, hardly breathing. The sound of barking came wafting on the night air.

'It's them,' said Josh. 'They're in the wood. It's only a matter of time before they'll be here.'

They lingered there in silence, uncertain which way to go. Suddenly a small creature darted through the undergrowth and out in front of them. High in the vault of trees above their heads, there was a shiver of powerful wings and something swooped.

Andy shone his torch and at the last moment an owl veered off to the right of them, soaring upwards and settling in the distant branches of a great tree. They stood watching it, entranced, and then it left its perch again and swooped over them so low they had to duck.

'Darn bird!' said Josh. 'What's it playing at?'

'I think it's trying to tell us something,' said Dame Lobelia as the owl swooped over for a third time.

'Yeah,' said Andy. 'That it doesn't like us.'

'The owl...' she mused. 'That's the hieroglyphic sign for "in".'

'Very interesting,' said Josh, glancing at the dark track behind them. 'But do you think that you could concentrate on trying to get us out of here?'

Dame Lobelia was unperturbed. She took the amulet from her pocket and studied it thoughtfully. It glowed, with a shimmering brightness, right through the linen handkerchief.

'"*Shen*..."' she mused, 'that's a word for "*tree*" in Egyptian...'

'We've got to get off this path,' insisted Josh. 'And quickly!'

'"In" and "tree",' she pondered. 'Hmmmm... "in" and "tree"...'

Suddenly she gasped. 'How could I have been so stupid? Andy, shine your torch on that tree over there – where the owl is!'

He did and he too gasped. 'It's the oak! I recognise that hollow half way up!'

'An owl's nest,' she explained. 'He's trying to tell us that the tunnel's in that tree!'

They stumbled, relieved, down the tunnel's mossy steps and into its enveloping silence. Walking steadily, too tense to speak, they fixed their eyes firmly on a point in the middle distance, straining for a first glimpse of the exit ahead.

But then, when the tunnel had made its final turn and they were almost at its end, they heard a sound. Vague and indistinct, it echoed up out of the dark behind them. They stopped to listen and it came again. The sound of voices. Louder now and rapidly getting louder.

They began to panic a little and quickened their pace almost to a run. Finally, they reached the steps and clambered up them and out into the trees. But when they got beyond the copse they froze.

Parked up on the grass verge a little way away was a car, shiny and black, the moonlight reflecting brightly off its dark-tinted windows. Sir Sebastian's limousine.

It took them a moment before they realised that there was no one in it.

'Lend me your penknife Andy. Quick!' hissed Dame Lobelia and she grabbed it eagerly from his grasp. 'Now, go to the barn – I won't be long.'

They hesitated, but she waved them on. 'Get going! NOW!'

In what felt like hours, but was really only a matter of minutes, she had joined them there.

'Open the doors wide!' she ordered and disappeared inside the barn. They dragged the doors apart and the next thing that they heard was the sound of an engine whirring into life. Two pools of brilliant light moved slowly forward and the Morris Minor came chugging out to meet them.

She yelled at them to jump in and they rattled down the track towards the road.

As they made the turn out of the field onto the tarmac, something was trapped in the glare of their headlights. A face, contorted with hatred and frustrated rage, loomed up out of the dark at them. They had to swerve to miss it. There was a squeal of brakes and the little car wobbled. Then it bucketed forward and seconds later the big black limousine went screeching after it.

'We've had it now,' said Josh.

'Don't be too sure of that,' said Dame Lobelia, her foot pressing the pedal almost to the floor.

'Are you kidding? That thing must be a three-litre job, at least.'

'I wouldn't know about that,' said Dame Lobelia. 'But it won't be going far on three flat tyres.'

'You mean you...?'

'I'm afraid I did. That penknife of yours was a godsend, Andy...Ah!' she was glancing in her mirror. 'I think you'll find they've stopped.'

The children turned to look through the rear window. The big black car had come to a halt in the middle of the road. Sir Sebastian had jumped out and was waving his fists at their departing back. It was the last time that they ever saw him.

Chapter 25

There were headlines in the newspapers for weeks. 'THE GREAT TOMB ROBBERY!' blared *The Trumpeter*, 'STOLEN MUMMY FOUND IN SECRET CHAMBER UNDER MILLIONAIRE'S MANSION.' 'ANONYMOUS CALLER TIPPED OFF POLICE,' disclosed *The News of the Globe*. And *The Sunday Probe* proclaimed: 'SEDGEWICK GONE TO GROUND: MISSING MILLIONAIRE COULD BE IN SOUTH AMERICA.'

The children read them all avidly, much to the annoyance of their father who could never find his paper when he wanted it.

As far as they could make out from the reports, someone – they suspected Dame Lobelia – had made an anonymous phone call to the police within hours of their escape from Sedgewick Hall.

The police had swooped immediately and discovered the underground chamber and a whole honeycomb of secret passageways. But the arch-villain himself had 'done a runner' and it was generally believed that he had managed to flee the country.

Since then almost four months had passed and in the meantime Dame Lobelia herself seemed to have disappeared. On several occasions they had cycled round to see her but she was never at home and the house always had a closed up, forsaken air.

In time, the events of the summer began to fade in the children's memories. Though there was a brief reminder of those worrying days one morning, in early November, when Gav uncovered a soil-encrusted spectacle case at the bottom of the garden. The excitement soon died down, however, since there was no sign of Freddie in it, not even the tiniest bone. And the general opinion in the family was that the cat next door had had him.

Now it was Christmas Eve and there was uproar and indignation in the Ridley household. This wasn't just because the chocolate decorations had all been snaffled off the Christmas tree and Mum was fed up about it. Or because the turkey (personally chosen and collected by Dad) looked like it was going to be too big to fit inside the oven. Or even because that very morning, much to her distress, Katie had discovered hidden in the cupboard under the stairs, a Santa's outfit, complete with beard (and boots exactly Dad's size).

No, what had really set the cat among the pigeons was something rather smaller than the turkey. But very much more alive.

That lunchtime the usual last-minute pile of Christmas cards had come tumbling through the letterbox. Then, after a brief pause, there had been a ring on the doorbell. Josh had gone to answer it, picking up the letters as he went. He had noticed that two were addressed to him and his heart had missed a beat when he recognised Melissa's handwriting on one of them. The other seemed to be from somewhere foreign.

Standing on the doorstep was a young man in a bright blue, official-looking uniform with a peaked cap. 'Ridley residence?' he said briskly. 'Mr William Ridley?'

'He's my dad,' said Josh.

'Delivery for you. Sign here, please.' He passed Josh his electronic signature pad and showed him where to sign.

'Thanks,' said the man and handed Josh the box. It was of blue cardboard, the same shade as the young man's uniform. It had a carrying handle on the top. Across its side it bore the words 'INTER-PET' and 'SAME DAY EXPRESS DELIVERIES'. And there was an envelope addressed to his father taped to it.

'What's this?' said Dad, peering crossly over his spectacles.

He had retreated to a corner of the living room where he was sitting reading the paper and trying to keep out of Mum's way. He had spent the better part of an exhausting morning attempting to find a smaller turkey. Unfortunately, it seemed that there wasn't one to be had for love or money in the whole of north-west London. When he had come back empty-handed Mum had exploded. She had thrown a packet of sage and onion at his head and with the words '*You* can stuff it then!' had stormed out of the kitchen. Now, just as he had settled down for a few minutes peace with *The Trumpeter* and a little drop of something alcoholic, he had been disturbed. He was far from pleased.

'It came for you just now,' said Josh, putting down the box in front of him.

Dad eyed it suspiciously. There were scratching noises coming from it. Gingerly he leaned forward and opened it. He peered inside. Two big brown eyes gazed back at him. In an instant their owner was up on its hind legs and covering Dad's hands with enthusiastic licks.

'A *puppy!*' squealed Katie, from the doorway. She ran towards the little creature and scooped it up in her arms.

Dad didn't speak. There was a mixture of bewilderment and outrage on his face.

Josh came to pet the dog as well. They put it on the floor and it ran around excitedly, leaping about and joyfully wagging its tiny tail.

'Why do I have the distinct feeling that this has got something to do with you three?' Dad's voice was dangerously calm.

The children opened their eyes wide and shrugged their shoulders. They had no idea. Andy, however, began to feel uneasy. There was something very familiar about the little dog. But he couldn't put his finger on quite what.

'There's a letter with it,' he said, pointing.

Dad peeled the envelope off the box, opened it and began to read. As he did so, his frown grew deeper and his mouth set in a thin, down-turned line. He glanced darkly over his glasses at the children. Then he began to read aloud.

'Dear William,

As you see, my gift for you this year is a rather unusual one. If you want to know whose fault it is you'd better ask your son. If he hadn't let Tickety-Boo go running off like that it would never have happened.

However, suffice it to say that just over eight weeks ago there was a happy event next door. There were five puppies in all. I would have sent you two had it not been for the vicar taking a liking to one of them. Someone else in the village has agreed to have another. So you can thank your lucky stars.

I have had to keep one myself and so has my neighbour. We are barely on speaking terms.

Season's Greetings,
Alice.

P.S. There is of course no question of a certificate from the Kennel Club. His mother is a mongrel.'

'Well, he's a lot better-looking than his father, at any rate,' said Mum, who had eavesdropped from the doorway.

'Oh, Mum, can we keep him? Can we?' cried Katie.

'Keep him? Of course we can't!' barked Dad. 'Are you stupid? He's going back right now. I'll take him there, myself!'

'Oh, no, no, no! I won't let you!' screeched Katie, in a state of utter anguish. 'If he goes, I'm going too!'

'Don't tempt me,' said Dad.

'He's really rather sweet, though, isn't he?' said Mum, stroking the little dog as he tried gently to chew the fingers of her other hand.

'Sweet!' exclaimed her husband, jumping up. 'I can't believe I'm hearing this! Have you forgotten what those blasted dogs did when Alice went to Spain?'

'Well, this one looks different. Rather nicer natured,' said Mum, giving the puppy a cuddle. Katie beamed.

'*Different?*' said Dad. 'What do you mean *different*? It's a *dog* isn't it?'

'Dogs aren't all the same, you know. Just like humans. Some have nice, reasonable temperaments and others…' Mum glared at her husband, 'don't.'

Exasperated, Mr Ridley turned on his sons. 'And which one of you was stupid enough to let that animal run off? It really was incredibly stupid!'

'Must run in the family,' Mum observed, 'on the father's side. Goes down the male line.'

'I couldn't help it…' Andy began weakly. He glanced up at his father's face, then saw that there was cause for hope. Mum's last remarks appeared to have taken the fight out of him.

'Well, please yourselves,' he fumed. 'I wash my hands of it.' He sat down abruptly and grabbed the paper. Then, pointedly ignoring everyone, he made a great display of reading it.

***

Half an hour later all was quiet on the parent front. Mum was in the kitchen, grappling with the turkey and Dad had been despatched to get two extra packs of stuffing and a bigger roasting tin before the shops shut.

The children were sitting on Josh's bedroom floor. Andy's 'DO NOT DISTURB' sign had been hung up on the outside of the door, just in case.

'Look,' said Josh, 'I think this is from Dame Lobelia.' He reached into his pocket and a Christmas card fluttered out onto the floor.

Andy picked it up. *'Dear Josh,'* he read out loud, *'thanks for the cool card and I hope you have a really great Christmas. Love from Melissa. PS see you at Siena's party on New Year's Eve.'*

Katie giggled.

'Not that!' said Josh, flushing to the roots of his hair and snatching the card out of his brother's hand. 'This.'

He held out a crumpled envelope. The others leaned forward to have a look. The handwriting on it was Dame Lobelia's, but the stamp was unfamiliar.

'It's from Egypt,' he said.

'Well, go on, read it then.'

Josh tore it open. Written at the top was: 'Mystic Nile Hotel, Luxor.' He cleared his throat and began to read:

'Greetings from Egypt my dear young friends!

I can't tell you how good it feels to be back! There's a new tomb been discovered in the Valley, so I'm here mixing business with pleasure. A combination of excavation and relaxation, I suppose you might call it.

I certainly felt like I needed a holiday after last summer. That final night at Sedgewick Hall left me severely shaken I don't mind telling you. When that thing came up out of the sarcophagus I thought I'd die of fright!

By the way, I looked it up in my Dictionary of Demonology when I got home. Turns out it was a Sekhmet demon. A particularly nasty type and usually lethal. It brings plague and pestilence and famine – which accounts for Josh having felt so ill, I suppose.

During that first week after everything was over, I thought about the amulet a lot. It seemed to me that, with Sedgewick still at large, we might go on needing its protection for many years to come.

If that were to be the case, I reasoned, I'd need to find a safer place to keep it than my little, semi-detached. I wracked my brains for days trying to think of somewhere and in the end I decided that there was only one place safe enough. A place so vast and empty, that even a man like Sedgewick would be defeated by it.

I took it back to Egypt – to the desert!

It took me weeks to find the perfect spot, but in the end I did. It was a cave, well off the camel track and far from any oasis, sheltered from the wind and sun. A place where only snakes and scorpions live. I buried it there, wrapped in my pocket-handkerchief, complete with all our names within its circle.

And there you have it my young friends! Now we can all sleep safely in our beds, secure in the knowledge that, should Sedgewick ever try to harm us, we'll be well protected. It's the best Christmas present any of us could ever have, I'm sure you will agree.

Yours, with all good wishes,
Lobelia Carter-Smythe.

P.S. In case you were wondering, it was me who made the phone call.'

When Josh had finished reading he sat silent for a moment lost in thought and no one spoke. It seemed an awe-inspiring notion! Buried somewhere in a remote cave, beneath the timeless sands of Egypt were their names, joined forever within a shining ring of stone, wrapped in Dame Lobelia's pocket-handkerchief.

In his mind Josh pictured her, majestic on a camel, sailing slowly through the desert like a stately ship. Or maybe in a dusty jeep, skimming across those wide, sun-scorched expanses. Or perhaps she slept by day to avoid the heat and travelled by night beneath the teeming stars…

'Two Christmas presents!' It was Katie who broke the silence. She sighed, gazing fondly down at the sleeping puppy in her lap. 'They're the best ones we've ever had! And it isn't even Christmas Day yet!'

The puppy woke up and yawned and stretched.

'What should we call him?' said Andy.

Josh glanced down at the letter in his hand and thought of Dame Lobelia: 'Let's call him *Shen*,' he said, 'to remind us all how lucky we've been.'

And everyone agreed that was an excellent suggestion.

About the Author

Susan Kassabian was born in North West London (where she still lives) and began writing while bringing up her two children. She has written short stories and a collection of humorous poems for children. The Mummy of Mulberry Avenue is her first novel.

Lightning Source UK Ltd.
Milton Keynes UK
UKOW050604010712

195306UK00001B/8/P